世界有时残酷 但爱从未缺席

［墨西哥］阿普里尔·温特斯 等 著

张白桦 译

真爱卷（中英双语）

世界微型小说精选

中国国际广播出版社

微型小说界的一个奇异存在

陈春水

张白桦，女，于1963年4月出生于辽宁沈阳一个世代书香的知识分子家庭，父亲是中国第一代俄语专业大学生。她曾先后就读于三所高校，具有双专业教育背景，所修专业分别为英国语言文学、比较文学与世界文学。她有两次跳级经历，一次是从初二到高三，另一次是从大一到大二。最后学历为上海外国语大学文学硕士，研究方向为译介学，师从谢天振教授（国际知名比较文学专家与翻译理论家、译介学创始人、中国翻译学创建人、比较文学终身奖获得者），为英美文学研究专家、翻译家胡允桓（与杨宪益、沙博理、赵萝蕤、李文俊、董乐山同获"中美文学交流奖"，诺贝尔文学奖得主托妮·莫里森世界范围内研究兼汉译第一人，翻译终身奖获得者）私淑弟子。她现为内蒙古工业大学外国语学院副教授、硕士研究生导师，并兼任中国比较文学学会翻译研究会理事、上海翻译家协会会员、内蒙古作家协会会员。张白桦于1987年开始文学创作,已在《读者》《中外期刊文萃》《青年博览》《小小说选刊》《青年参考》《文学故事报》等海内外一百多种报刊,以及生活·读书·新知三联书店、中译出版社、北京大学出版社、中国国际广播出版社,公开出版以微型小说翻译为主,包括长篇小说、中篇小说、散文、随笔、诗歌、杂文、评论翻译和原创等在内的编著译作36部,累计1200万字。

在中国微型小说界,众所周知的是:以性别而论,男性译作者多,女性译作者少;以工作内容而论,搞创作的多,搞研究的少;以文学样式而论,只创作微型小说的作者多,同时创作长篇小说、散文、诗歌、文学评论的作者少;以作者性质而论,搞原创的多,搞翻译的少;以翻译途径而论,外译汉的译者多,汉译外的译者少;以译者而论,搞翻译的人多,同时搞原创的人少。而具备上述所有"少"于一身的奇异存在,恐怕张白桦是绝无仅有的一位。

张白桦是当代中国微型小说第一代译作者,也是唯一因微型小说翻译而获奖的翻译家。其译作量大质优,覆盖面广泛,风格鲜明,具有女性文学史、微型小说史意义;是中国第一个从理论上,从宏观和微观层面,论证当代外国微型小说汉译的文学史意义的学者,具有翻译文学史意义;小说创作篇幅涉及长篇、中篇、短篇、微型小说,创作的文学样式覆盖小说、散文、诗歌、文学评论等主要文学样式;是既有微型小说译作,又有微型小说原创的全能型译作家，且译作与原创具有通约性；还是微型小说英汉双向翻译的译者。她的微型小说翻译实践开创了中国微型小说双向翻译的两个"第一"："译趣坊"系列图书为中国首部微型小说译文集，在美国出版的《凌鼎年微型小说选集》为中国首部微型小说自选集英译本。

2002年，其微型小说译著《英汉经典阅读系列散文卷》曾获上海外国语大学研究生学术文化节科研成果奖；1998年，其微型小说译作《爱旅无涯》获《中国青年报·青年参考》最受读者喜爱的翻译文学作品；她本人曾在2001年当选小小说存档作家、2002年当选为当代微型小说百家；微型小说译作《仇家》当选为全国第四次微型小说续写大赛竞赛原作；2012年，其译作《海妖的诱惑》获以色列第32届世界诗人大会主席奖等文学奖项；"译趣坊"系列图书深受广大青年读者喜欢。

此外，她的论文《外国微型小说在中国的初期接受》入选复旦大学出版社的《润物有声——谢天振教授七十华诞纪念文集》，以及湖南大学出版社的张春的专著《中国小小说六十年》续表。译作《门把手》入选春风文艺出版社出版的《21世纪中国文学大系2002年翻译文学》。译作《生命倒计时》入选春风文艺出版社出版的谢天振、韩忠良的专著《21世纪中国文学大系2010年翻译文学》。

张白桦关于外国微型小说的论文具有前沿性和开拓意义。例如，《外国微型小说在中国的初期接受》是国内对于外国微型小说在中国接受的宏观梳理和微观分析。《当代外国微型小说汉译的文学史意义》证实了"微型小说翻译与微型小说原创具有同样建构民族、国别文学发展史的意义，即翻译文学应该，也只能是中国文学的一部分"。她指出，当代外国微型小说汉译的翻译文学意义在于："推动中国当代的主流文学重归文学性，重归传统诗学的'文以载道'的传统；引进并推动确立了一种新型的、活力四射的文学样式；当代微型小说汉译提高了文学的地位，直接催生并参与改写了中国当代文学史，以一种全新的文体重塑了当代主流诗学。"

其论文也反映出张白桦的文学翻译观和文学追求，例如，在《外国微型小说在中国的初期接受》中，她说："吾以吾手译吾心。以文化和文学的传播为翻译的目的，以妇女儿童和青年为目标读者，让国人了解世界上其他民族的妇女儿童和青年的生存状态。以'归化'为主，'异化'为辅的翻译策略，全译为主，节译和编译为辅，突出译作的影响作用和感化作用，从而形成了简洁隽永、抒情、幽默、时尚的翻译风格。与此同时，译作与母语原创的微型小说，在思想倾向、语言要素、风格类型和审美趣味上形成了通约性和文化张力，丰富了译作的艺术表现力和感染力。"

在《当代外国微型小说汉译的文学史意义》中，她说："文学翻译是创造性叛逆，创造性叛逆赋予原作以第二次生命。处于文学样式'真空状态'的中国第一代微型小说译者一方面充分发挥了翻译的主体性作用，挥洒着'创造性叛逆'所带来的'豪杰'范儿，对于原文和原语文化'傲娇'地'引进并抵抗着',有意和无意地遵循着自己的文学理想和审美趣味'舞蹈'着,为翻译文学披上了'中国红'的外衣,在内容和形式上赋予译作一种崭新的面貌和第二次生命。一方面在原文、意识形态、经济利益、诗学观念的'镣铐'上,'忠实'并'妥协'着。"

著名评论家张锦贻在《亭亭白桦秀译林》中说:"张白桦所译的作品范围极广,涉及世界各大洲,但选择的标准却极严,注重原作表现生活的力度和反映社会的深度。显然,张白桦对于所译原作的这种选择,绝不仅仅是出于爱好,而是反映出她的审美意识和情感倾向。她着力在译作中揭示不同地区、不同国度、不同社会、不同人种的生存境况和心理状态,揭示东西方之间的文化差异和分歧,都显示出她是从人性和人道的角度来观察现实的人生。而正是通过这样的观察,才使她能够真正地去接触各国文学中那些反映社会底层的大众作品,才能使她真正地关注儿童和青年,也才使她的译作真正地走向中国的民众。事实证明,译作的高品位必伴以译者识见的高明和高超。脱了思想内核,怕是做不好文学译介工作的。……类似的译作比比皆是,到后来,就是事先不知道译者,几行读下来,亦能将她给'认出来'。也就是说,张白桦在选择原作和自己的翻译文字上都在逐步形成一种独具的风格。……使她能够在不同的译作中巧用俚语,活用掌故,借用时俗。她善于用中国人最能领会的词语来表达各式各样的口吻,由此活现出不同人物的身份和此时此刻的心神和表情；她也长于用青少年最能领悟的词句来表达不同的侧面，同时展现出不同社会的氛围和当时当地的风习。"

胡晓在《中国教育报》发表的《学英语您捕捉到快乐了吗》中说："我最喜欢她的译作，因为所选篇目均为凝练精巧之作，难易适中，且多是与生活息息相关的内容，能够极大限度地接近读者。所选的文字皆为沙里淘金的名家经典，文华高远，辞采华丽。名家的经典带来的是审美的享受和精神的愉悦，含蓄隽永的语句令人不由得会心一笑；至真至纯的爱与情，轻轻拨动着人们的神经；睿智透彻的思考，让人旷达而超脱。"

综上所述，在微型小说的文化地理中，张白桦是一个独特的所在。她以独特的文化品相，承接了中华与西洋的博弈，以理论和实践造就的衍生地带，自绘版图却无人能袭。

（作者系中国作协会员，小小说作家网特约评论家，第六届小小说金麻雀提名奖获得者，本篇原载于中国作家网2015年9月9日。网址：http://www.chinawriter.com.cn）

没有微型小说汉译就没有当代微型小说

——张白桦访谈录

陈勇（中国作协会员，小小说作家网特约评论家，第六届小小说金麻雀提名奖获得者，以下简称陈）：我做微型小说评论多年，范围遍及世界华文微型小说界，您是我研究视野中出现的第一个微型小说翻译家，可能也是唯一的一个。

张白桦（以下简称张）：谢谢陈老师的青睐，我更加惊诧于您的学术识别力。因为，即使在外语界和翻译界，对于文学翻译的认识还是有许多误区的。难怪微型小说界的评论总是视译者为"局外人"，所以无人问津了。而从我的研究方向——译介学的角度来看，得出的结论是：微型小说翻译，特别是微型小说翻译文学，应该，也只是中国文学的一部分。

陈：我认同翻译与创作是国别文学的"鸟之两翼，车之两轮"之说。您能给大家普及一下文学翻译与文学创作的区别吗？

张：好的，我愿意。从文艺的本质规律来看，二者并没有分别。

从创作的内容来看,翻译的确比创作少了一道工序——构思。然而,也正是由于这一缺失,反而给翻译带来了创作所没有的困难。可以负责任地说,从创作的过程来看,正如许许多多20世纪三四十年代的作家兼翻译家共同体会到的那样,文学翻译比文学创作要难。

陈:我之所以选择了您作为评论对象,是由于您在微型小说界的独特地位和影响力,以及您在研究和实践层面全面开花的成果。

张:这倒是符合事实的。在实践方面,我在20世纪80年代初,也就是大三的时候,就翻译了第一篇微型小说,一直走下来,应该说与当代中国微型小说是共同成长的,又是唯一一个因此获奖的译者;此外,中国首部微型小说译文集"译趣坊"系列图书和中国首部微型小说自选集英译本《凌鼎年微型小说选集》也是我做的。在研究方面,是中国第一个从理论上,从宏观和微观层面,论证当代外国微型小说汉译的文学史意义的学人。

陈:您能把您的理论观点论述得详细些吗?

张:可以。当代外国微型小说汉译的翻译文学意义就在于:推动中国当代的主流文学重归文学性,重归传统诗学的"文以载道"的传统;引进并推动确立了一种新型的、活力四射的文学样式;当代微型小说汉译提高了文学的地位,直接催生并参与改写了中国当代文学史,以一种全新的文体重塑了当代主流诗学。

陈:哦,所以您才会下这样的判断:"没有外国微型小说汉译,就没有当代微型小说。"是吗?

张：您的学术敏感度令人惊叹。

陈：根据我的调查统计分析，发现搞微型小说翻译实践的人虽然相对不多，却也还是有一些的。您能谈谈使您脱颖而出的"别裁之处"吗？

张：我是经历了实践—理论—再实践这样一个非线性的过程，它带给我的是对文学翻译本质的思考，对翻译艺术掌控力的把握，对文学翻译的全面观照。据我所知，微型小说译者的文化背景比较复杂，创作态度也良莠不齐。老一辈翻译家在语言文化基础和创作态度上是无可厚非的，基本表现为"全译"，可惜在文字上与原文"靠得太近"，人数也太少；中青年译者的数量居多，但语言文化基础大多不如前辈，在对原文的处理上"尺度过大"，多数表现为"编译"。

我生性保守，为人为文拘谨，记得曾经在《世界华文微型小说作家微自传》中这样总结过："回首往事，也算是'张三中'吧：'心中'的原文，'眼中'的译文，'意中'的师生。"换句话说，对原文的敬畏，对译文的时代化，对青年、妇女儿童读者的念念不忘，千方百计地贴近时代，可能因此造就我的译文忠实性和可读性较强，基本表现为"全译"。

陈：果然如此。在您的译作中，我发现有几个题材是您情有独钟的，比如，青年、妇女和儿童。也就是说，这是您自觉的文学追求，是您的"主观倾向"吧？

张：您一语中的。是的，身为女性，我"含泪的微笑"更多地落在了相似群体身上，是希望通过译作擦亮人文关怀的"镜与灯"。

陈：如果让您用几个关键词来概括您的翻译风格的话，您会选择哪些词？

张：首先进入我脑海的是：简洁、幽默、时尚。

陈：为什么是这三个词，而不是其他？

张：这个嘛，都源于我的"本色演出"。我这人简单直接，译文也就长不了；身为教书匠，我喜欢寓教于乐，译文也就搞文字狂欢；我的目标读者是青年，我的译文就各种"潮"，"一大波流行词语正在靠近"。

陈：嗯嗯，听出来啦。最后，我还是要不客气地指出您在创作趋势上的一个问题：您的微型小说翻译在初期量大质优，"凡有井水处，皆能歌柳词"，而近期在数量上却大不如前了，希望您可以有所弥补。

张：谢谢陈老师指教，我也意识到了这个问题。原因是多方面的，最重要的还是我目前的长篇著译、教学和研究生辅导让我分身乏术。不过，我一定竭尽心力，在理论上继续为微型小说翻译"鼓与呼"，在实践上做"颜色不一样的烟火"。

（本篇原载于中国作家网 2015 年 9 月 9 日。网址：http://www.chinawriter.com.cn）

目 录

没商量 / No Wiggle Room · 1

黑衣女人 / The Lady in Black · 6

爱情 / Love · 19

见鬼 / Astral Ankith · 22

玫瑰的玫瑰 / Roses for Rose · 36

那只最后的蝴蝶 / The Last Butterfly · 41

儿子理发 / David's Haircut · 48

叉子掉了 / The Fork Dropped · 57

查尔斯 / Charles · 65

离开比尔 / Leaving Bill · 74

老照片 / The Photograph · 91

黑色面纱 / Black Veil · 98

一个小奇迹 / A Small Miracle · 110

维内诺上尉求婚 / Captain Veneno's Proposal of Marriage · 117

衬衫夫人的回忆 / Mrs.Blouse's Memories · 129

黑洞之旅 / The Cave · 133

大大的惊喜 / A Big Surprise · 143

校园霸凌者 / The Bully · 150

回家的感觉真好 / Being Back Home · 159

他的青春期就这样结束了 / His Youth Came to an End · 163

她留下了她的鞋 / She Left Her Shoes · 174

援助之手 / A Helping Hand · 179

碧波倒影里的爱情 / Angela, An Inverted Love Story · 186

一天的等待 / A Day's Wait · 200

机器人保姆 / BERTIE · 211

译后记 · 225

没商量

[墨西哥]阿普里尔·温特斯

莱妮坐在那儿盯着那封没拆开的信封,她长叹一声,把包裹撕开,让里面的东西溜到厨房的柜台上。

三个小时后,她拿着信封走进餐厅,身材看上去比墨西哥胡椒还要辣。黑色的卷发从她的脖子上披散下来,香槟色的蕾丝连衣裙和她奶油色的皮肤浑然一体,每个人都转过头来向她行注目礼……除了那两个人。

莱妮大步走到一个雅座前,那里坐着一男一女,靠得很近,低声交谈着。她丈夫抬起头时,莱妮亲眼看着他脸上的血色渐渐消失,他睁大眼睛,结结巴巴地说:"莱妮!你……你在这儿干什么?"

和她丈夫在一起的那个女人用怀疑的目光盯着莱妮。

这么说,这个恶棍没有费心告诉这个女人他结婚了,莱妮想。

她再回头看汤姆时,她的脸上满是厌恶。"我很庆幸我坚持婚前不忠条款适用于你我双方。感谢你让这一切变得容易。"

"等一下,莱妮。玛戈和我只是一起吃商务晚餐……一个监督会议,仅此而已。你没有理由产生误会,宝贝。"

玛戈被水呛到了,她缓过来后怒视着汤姆,"你可没有提到你结婚了,我觉得这真的是一次监督会议!"她拿起钱包,溜出雅座,转身向门口走去。

汗水顺着汤姆的太阳穴往下流,但他是个律师,一个惯于用言语逃避一切的人。正如莱妮所料,他露出了最迷人的笑容,目光从她脸上移开,扫视着她身体的曲线。"我以前从未见过这件衣服,你今晚看起来棒极了!"

他真的认为自己是那么有魅力,她无论如何都会原谅他吗?莱妮在那一刻意识到,她的确嫁给了一个混蛋。

她挺起胸膛,怒目而视,说道:"去跟我的律师说吧。"

"可是,亲爱的,你不明白……"

"别叫我'亲爱的',汤姆,"莱妮打断说。"我比你还要明白。"她把照片扔在桌子上,有些落在了还没吃完的甜点上。

汤姆把酒吐了出来。

莱妮拿起其中一张照片瞥了一眼。"连我都得必须承认玛戈穿着红色胸罩和内裤看起来很性感。你看,你的手摸遍了她的全身。"

汤姆把手指放在脖子和衬衫之间,然后用力拉,好像有人要勒死他似的。

莱妮的眼里满是伤心。"不幸的是,你无法用言语来解决这个问题。一切都结束了,汤姆。"

No Wiggle Room

By April Winters

Lainie sat staring at the unopened envelope. She let out a long sigh, sliced the package open, and slid the contents out onto the kitchen counter.

Three hours later, envelope in hand, she entered the restaurant looking hotter than a jalapeno. Dark curls swept up off her neck, her dress of champagne-colored lace blended with her creamy skin. She turned every head in the place...except two.

Lainie strode over to a booth where a man and woman sat in close contact, quietly conversing. When her husband looked up, Lainie watched the color drain from his face. His eyes widened, and he sputtered, "Lainie! Wha...what are you doing here?"

The woman he was with turned questioning eyes on Lainie.

So, the rotten bastard didn't bother to tell you he's married, Lainie thought.

Her face was filled with disgust when she looked back at Tom. "I'm certainly glad I insisted that prenup infidelity clause apply to both of us. Thanks for making this easy."

"Now wait a minute, Lainie. Margo and I were just having a business dinner…an oversight meeting, that's all. There's no reason for you to jump to the wrong conclusion, baby."

Margo gagged on her water. When she recovered, she glared at Tom. "You didn't mention you were married. I guess this really was an oversight meeting!" She picked up her purse, slid out of the booth, turned and headed for the door.

Sweat trickled down Tom's temple, but he was a lawyer, a man used to talking his way out of anything. Just as Lainie expected, he put on his most charming grin. His eyes slid from her face to roam the curves of her body. "I've never seen that dress before. You look fabulous tonight!"

Did he really think he was so irresistible she'd forgive him no matter what? Lainie realized in that moment there was no denying she'd married a scumbag.

She squared her shoulders, glared, and said, "Tell it to my attorney."

"But, honey, you don't understand…"

"Don't 'honey' me, Tom," Lainie interrupted. "And I understand more than you know." She dumped the photographs on the table, some of them landing in the unfinished dessert.

Tom spewed his wine.

Lainie picked up one of the pictures and gave it a glance.

"Even I have to admit Margo looks pretty sultry in that red bra and panties. And look, your hands are all over her."

Tom stuck his finger between his neck and shirt then tugged as if someone were strangling him.

Lainie's eyes filled with sadness. "Unfortunately you're not going to be able to talk your way out of this one. It's over, Tom."

黑衣女人

[美国]埃莉诺·H.波特

房子里鸦雀无声。门廊那边的小房间里,有位穿黑色衣服的女士独自坐着。在她旁边,一件白色的童装搭在椅子上。在她脚下的地板上,放着一双小小的鞋子。一个洋娃娃搭在椅子上,一张床架上摆着一只玩具士兵。

四处都静悄悄的——时钟都停止了嘀嗒,对于一间房间来说,这么安静很奇怪。

时钟放在床尾的书架上。穿黑色衣服的女人看着它。她记起三个月前的那天晚上,当愤怒的浪涛袭向她的时候,她伸出手关掉了时钟。

从那以后它一直都静悄悄的,它也应该静悄悄的。现在,时间嘀嘀嗒嗒地流逝还会有什么用呢?正如小凯瑟琳面色苍白地躺在那里,被掩埋在黑土之下,还会有什么更要紧的事呢?

"妈妈!"

黑衣女人不安地动了一下,看向那扇关着的门。她知道在门后面有个长着一对蓝色大眼睛的小男孩需要她。但是她不希望他叫她妈妈。

这只会让她想起另两片薄薄的嘴唇——那两片现在再也不能说话的嘴唇。

"妈妈！"那个声音更大了。

黑衣女人没有应答。她想如果她不应答的话，小男孩可能会走开。

短暂的寂静过后，门慢慢地打开了。

"呀！"一种高兴的、发现一个人之后的喊叫，但随后归于寂静。面无笑容的女人没有让他靠近。小男孩第一步迈得很小心。

然后小男孩停住了脚步，小心翼翼地说："我在这里。"

这可能是他说过的最不讨喜的话，因为这让黑衣女人更痛苦地想起另一个小孩已经不在了。她发出一声尖利的喊叫，然后用手捂住了脸。

"鲍比，鲍比。"她哭了出来，释放出一种不可思议的悲伤。"走开！走开！我想一个人待着——一个人！"

男孩脸上的光彩消失了。他的眼睛流露出被深深伤害的神情。他等着，但是她没动。小男孩轻声抽泣着离开了房间。

过了好一会儿，黑衣女人抬起头，透过窗子看到了小男孩。他和他的父亲在院子里的苹果树下玩。

玩！

黑衣女人用严肃的眼神看着他们，嘴角的线条生硬起来。

鲍比有人和他玩，有人爱他，照顾他，然而在那个山坡上，凯瑟琳是孤独的——完全孤独的。

黑衣女人轻轻地叫了一声，跳了起来，然后匆忙回到自己的房间。当她把黑色面纱别在帽子上遮住自己的时候，她的手都在颤抖。但是当她下楼穿过大厅时，她的脚步是坚定的。

苹果树下的男人急忙站起走上前来。

"海伦，最亲爱的——今天就不要再这样啦！"他哀求道。"亲爱的，这没有用的！"

"可是她孤独一人——是完全孤独的。你都不想想！没人会想——没人了解我的感觉。你不懂我。你懂我的话，就会跟我来，就不会要我留下来——留在这里！"女人哽咽道。

"我一直都跟你在一起，亲爱的，"男人温柔地说，"我今天跟你在一起，自从她离开我们以后，我差不多每天都跟你在一起，但是，这没有用——在她的坟头没完没了地哀悼。这只会让你、我和鲍比更难过。鲍比在——这里，你也是知道的，亲爱的！"

"不，不要这么说，"女人疯狂地喊道，"你不懂！你不懂！"她转身急匆匆地走了，留下男人目送着她，眼里全是担心，男孩的眼里全是难过。

到坟地的路并不长。黑衣女人知道路。尽管如此，她还是跌跌撞撞的，伸出手来乱抓。她倒在一块标有"凯瑟琳"的小石碑前。在她旁边，有一位白发苍苍的女人，双手握着满满一把粉红色和白色的玫瑰，同情地看着她。白发苍苍的女人顿了顿，张开嘴巴，好像要说些什么。接着她转过身来，开始摆放旁边墓上的鲜花。

黑衣女人抬起了头，有那么一会儿，她只是默默地看着，然后，她掀开面纱，说："你也关心。"她轻轻地说道："你懂。我以前在这里也见过你。你的亲人——是一个小女孩？"

白发苍苍的女人摇了摇头。"不是的，亲爱的，是一个小男孩——或者说，他四十年前是一个小男孩。"

"四十年——这么长时间！没有了他，你这四十年是怎么熬过来的？"

白发苍苍的瘦小女人这次又摇了摇头。"人有时——不得不，亲爱的，不过，这个小男孩不是我的儿子。"

"可是你关心，你懂。我以前也常常看见你到这里来。"

"是的，你看，那是因为再也没有人关心，曾经有一个人关心过，而现在是我，代表她，关心了。"

"代表她？"

"代表他母亲。"

"哦——哦！"黑衣女人轻轻地叫了一声，声音里是随之而来的同情。黑衣女人的目光落到了标有"凯瑟琳"的墓碑上。

"倒不是我不了解她的感觉，"白发苍苍的女人说道，"你看，出事的时候我是男孩的护士，后来我在这家干了很多年，所以我是了解的。我目睹了这件事的整个过程，从小男孩遭遇意外开始。"

"意外！"凯瑟琳的母亲叫了一声，声音里满是关心和同情。

"是的，是马失控，他两天后死亡。"

"我知道！我知道！"黑衣女人哽咽着说，不过，她此时想的不是男孩和马失控意外事件。

"从那时候开始，我女主人的一切都停止了，"白发苍苍的女人继续说道，"从头到尾。她还有一个丈夫和一个女儿，可是似乎这对她来说都不重要了——哪个都不重要了。除了这里——这座小坟，什么都不重要了。她到坟前来，一待就是几个小时，带着鲜花来，对着坟自言自语。"

黑衣女人突然抬起头来，盯着白发苍苍的女人的脸。

白发苍苍的女人接着说道："家里的气氛越来越悲伤，而她似乎并不在意，似乎她就想要这样的气氛。她遮挡阳光，把照片收起来，她只在儿子的房间里呆坐，那里的一切陈设都还是他离开前的样子，她什么都不让动。我后来猜测她知不知道这样做会带来什么后果，可是她确实不知道。"

"'后果'？"黑衣女人的声音在颤抖。

"是的,我纳闷她有没有看出她在失去他们——她的丈夫和女儿,可是她确实没看出来。"

黑衣女人一动不动地坐着。好像鸟儿也停止了歌唱。白发苍苍的女人继续说道:"你看,所以,我才会来这里献花,是代表她,除了她,现在没有人关心。"她幽幽长叹,站起身来。

"可是你还没讲完——发生了什么事?"黑衣女人轻轻地说道。

"实际上我自己也不明白。我知道男人离开了。他四处游荡,像旅游似的,不常在家。当他回来的时候看起来像有病的样子,情绪也很糟糕。他回家的次数越来越少,最后他死了。不过那是在她死了之后。他就埋在那里,在她和儿子的旁边。女儿——没有人知道她在哪里。女孩喜欢花、阳光、欢笑和年轻人,你知道的,她家里一样没有。我猜测,所以她就走了——去能找到这些的地方了。"

"你看,如果我不走的话,就会继续把你拴在这和我说话!"白发苍苍的瘦小女人带着歉意说道。

"不,不。我很高兴听你讲。"黑衣女人说,摇摇晃晃地站起来。她的脸变得苍白,从她的眼里能看到突如其来的恐惧。"我必须得走了。谢谢你。"她掉转头,急匆匆地走了。

当黑衣女人到家的时候,房子仍然静悄悄的。她因这寂静而颤抖。她赶紧上楼,心有愧疚。在她自己的房间里,她取下罩在脸上的面纱,哭了起来,轻声的哭泣中夹杂着哽咽和含混不清的话。当她脱下黑衣的时候,还在哭。

过了一会儿,女人——不再穿黑衣服了——慢慢地走下楼去。她的眼里还有泪光,但是双唇却勇敢地弯成了一个微笑的模样。她穿上了一件白衣,头上插了一支白玫瑰。在她后面,穿过走廊的小房间里,那靠近床尾架子上的小小的时钟大声地嘀嗒着。

楼下的大厅里传来跑步的声音,然后是一个男孩高兴的声音:
"妈妈!是妈妈回来了!"
随着一声小声的哭泣,男孩的母亲对她的儿子张开了双臂。

The Lady in Black

By Eleanor H.Porter

The house was very still. In the little room over the porch, the lady in Black sat alone. Near her, a child's white dress lay across a chair. On the floor at her feet lay a tiny pair of shoes. A doll hung over a chair and a toy soldier occupied the little stand by the bed.

And everywhere was silence—the strange silence that comes only to a room where the clock has stopped ticking.

The clock stood on the shelf near the end of the bed. The Lady in Black looked at it. She remembered the wave of anger that had come over her when she had reached out her hand and silenced the clock that night three months before.

It had been silent ever since and it should remain silent, too. Of what possible use were the hours it would tick away now? As if anything mattered, with little Kathleen lying out there white and still under the black earth!

"Muvver!"

The Lady in Black moved restlessly and looked toward the

closed door. Behind it, she knew, was a little boy with wide blue eyes who wanted her. But she wished he would not call her by that name.

It only reminded her of those other little lips—silent now.

"Muvver!" The voice was more demanding.

The Lady in Black did not answer. He might go away, she thought, if she did not answer.

There was a short silence, and then the door opened slowly.

"Pe-eek!" It was a cry of joyful discovery, but it was followed almost immediately by silence. The unsmiling woman did not invite him to come near. The boy was unsteady at his first step.

He paused, then spoke carefully, "I's—here."

It was maybe the worst thing he could have said. To the Lady in Black it was a yet more painful reminder of that other one who was not there. She gave a sharp cry and covered her face with her hands.

"Bobby, Bobby," she cried out, in a release of unreasoning sadness. "Go away! Go away! I want to be alone—alone!"

All the brightness fled from the boy's face. His eyes showed a feeling of deep hurt. He waited, but she did not move. Then, with a half-quieted cry, he left the room.

Long minutes afterward, the Lady in Black raised her head and saw him through the window. He was in the yard with his father, playing under the apple tree.

Playing!

The Lady in Black looked at them with serious eyes, and her mouth hardened at the corners.

Bobby had someone to play with him, someone to love him and care for him, while out there on the hillside Kathleen was alone—all alone.

With a little cry the Lady in Black sprang to her feet and hurried into her own room. Her hands shook as she pinned on her hat and covered herself with her black veil. But her step was firm as she walked downstairs and out through the hall.

The man under the apple tree rose hurriedly and came forward.

"Helen, dearest—not again, today!" he begged. "Darling, it can't do any good!"

"But she's alone—all alone. You don't seem to think! No one thinks—no one knows how I feel. You don't understand. If you did, you'd come with me. You wouldn't ask me to stay—here!" choked the woman.

"I have been with you, dear," said the man gently. "I've been with you today, and every day, almost, since—since she left us. But it can't do any good—this continuous mourning over her grave. It only makes more sadness for you, for me, and for Bobby. Bobby is—here, you know, dear!"

"No, no, don't say it," cried the woman wildly. "You don't understand! You don't understand!" And she turned and hurried away, followed by the worried eyes of the man, and the sad eyes of the boy.

It was not a long walk to the burial place. The Lady in Black knew the way. Yet, she stumbled and reached out blindly. She fell before a little stone marked "Kathleen". Near her a gray-haired woman, with her hands full of pink and white roses, watched her sympathetically. The gray-haired woman paused and opened her lips as if she would speak. Then she turned slowly and began to arrange her flowers on a grave nearby.

The Lady in Black raised her head. For a time she watched in silence. Then she threw back her veil and spoke, "You care, too," she said softly. "You understand. I've seen you here before, I'm sure. And was yours —a little girl?"

The gray-haired woman shook her head. "No, dearie, it's a little boy—or he was a little boy forty years ago."

"Forty years—so long! How could you have lived forty years—without him?"

Again the little woman shook her head. "One has to—sometimes, dearie, but this little boy wasn't mine."

"But you care. You understand. I've seen you here so often before."

"Yes. You see, there's no one else to care. But there was once, and I'm caring now, for her sake."

"For her?"

"His mother."

"Oh-h!" It was a tender little cry, full of quick sympathy. The eyes of the Lady in Black were on the stone marked "Kathleen".

"It ain't as if I didn't know how she'd feel," said the gray-haired woman. "You see, I was nurse to the boy when it happened, and for years afterward I worked in the family. So I know. I saw the whole thing from the beginning, from the very day when the little boy here met with the accident."

"Accident!" It was a cry of concern and sympathy from Kathleen's mother.

"Yes. It was a runaway and he didn't live two days."

"I know! I know!" choked the Lady in Black. Yet she was not thinking of the boy and the runaway horse accident.

"Things stopped then for my mistress," continued the little gray-haired woman, "and that was the beginning of the end. She had a husband and a daughter, but they didn't seem to be important—not either of 'em. Nothin' seemed important except this little grave out here. She came and spent hours over it, bringin' flowers and talkin' to it."

The Lady in Black raised her head suddenly and quickly looked into the woman's face.

The woman went on speaking. "The house got sadder and sadder, but she didn't seem to mind. She seemed to want it so. She shut out the sunshine and put away many of the pictures. She sat only in the boy's room. And there, everything was just as it was when he left it. She wouldn't let a thing be touched. I wondered afterward that she didn't see where it was all leading to, but she didn't."

"'Leading to'?" The voice shook.

"Yes. I wondered she didn't see she was losing them—that husband and daughter; but she didn't see it."

The Lady in Black sat very still. Even the birds seemed to have stopped their singing. Then the gray-haired woman spoke: "So, you see, that's why I come and put flowers here. It's for her. There's no one else now to care." she sighed, rising to her feet.

"But you haven't told yet—what happened?" said the Lady in Black, softly.

"I don't know myself really. I know the man went away. He got somethin' to do travelin' so he wasn't home much. When he did come he looked sick and bad. He come less and less, and he died. But that was after she died. He's buried over there beside her and the boy. The girl—well, nobody knows where the girl is. Girls like flowers and sunshine and laughter and young people, you know, and she didn't get any of them at home. So she went—where she did get 'em, I suppose."

"There, and if I haven't gone and tired you all out with my talkin'!" said the little gray-haired woman regretfully.

"No, no. I was glad to hear it," said the Lady in Black, rising unsteadily to her feet. Her face had grown white, and her eyes showed a sudden fear. "But I must go now. Thank you." And she turned and hurried away.

The house was very still when the Lady in Black reached home. She shivered at its silence. She hurried up the stairs, almost with guilt. In her own room she pulled at the dark veil that covered her face. She was crying now, a choking little cry with broken words running through it. She was still crying as she removed her black dress.

Long minutes later, the Lady—in black no longer—moved slowly down the stairway. Her eyes showed traces of tears, but her lips were bravely curved in a smile. She wore a white dress and a single white rose in her hair. Behind her, in the little room over the porch, a tiny clock ticked loudly on its shelf near the end of the bed.

There came a sound of running feet in the hall below, then:

"Muvver!—it's Muvver come back!" shouted a happy voice.

And with a little sobbing cry Bobby's mother opened her arms to her son.

爱 情

[英国]托马斯·布朗

我爱你,不是因为你是一个怎样的人,而是因为我喜欢与你在一起时的感觉。

没有人值得你流泪,值得让你流泪的人不会让你哭泣。

思念某人,最糟糕的莫过于,近在身旁,却犹如远在天边。

纵然伤心,也不要愁眉不展,因为你不知谁会爱上你的笑容。

对于世界而言,你可能只是一个人;但是对于某人,你可能是他的整个世界。

不要在那些不愿在你身上花费时间的男人或者女人身上浪费你的时间。

爱你的人如果没有按你所希望的方式爱你,那并不代表他们没有全心全意地爱你。

不要心急火燎,最好的总会在最不经意间闪现。

在遇到真命天子之前,上天也许会安排我们先遇到别人;当我们终于遇见真命天子时,才会懂得心存感激。

不要因为结束而哭泣,微笑吧,为你的曾经拥有。

生命是一束纯净的火焰,我们依靠虽不可见却存于内心的太阳而存在。

Love

By Thomas Browne

I love you not because of who you are, but because of who I am when I am with you.

No man or woman is worth your tears, and the one who is, won't make you cry.

The worst way to miss someone is to be sitting right beside them knowing you can't have them.

Never frown, even when you are sad, because you never know who is falling in love with your smile.

To the world you may be one person, but to one person you may be the world.

Don't waste your time on a man or woman, who isn't willing to waste their time on you.

Just because someone doesn't love you the way you want them to, doesn't mean they don't love you with all they have.

Don't try too hard, the best things come when you least expect them to.

Maybe God wants us to meet a few wrong people before meeting the right one, so that when we finally meet the person, we will know how to be grateful.

Don't cry because it is over, smile because it happened.

Life is a pure flame, and we live by an invisible sun within us.

见 鬼

[印度]戈塔姆·甘尼什，亚什旺特·斯里寒兰

他已经死了好几分钟了，如果人们可以称之为死的话。安基斯坐在自己旁边，看着自己那一动不动、毫无生气的身体，被一种麻木感吞噬了。他感觉就像是同时有一百万种思绪在他的大脑中闪过，却一种也没有留住。他想知道是否还能称它为他的大脑，毕竟用凡人的话说，他只是一个鬼而已。

安基斯看了看他自己。不确定自己究竟是不是一个鬼。他没有形态，甚至没有轮廓。他看不到自己，甚至不确定是否他能看见东西，因为他没有眼睛。他所能感受到的一切是自己的存在感，是显灵的灵魂。但是那个男人——悬崖下的那个男人——安基斯见过他，他是半透明的——难道他原本是——这可能吗？安基斯大惑不解。

安基斯还清晰地记着事情是怎么发生的。当时他和哥哥还有哥哥的朋友们正在玩板球。那是暑假的一天，一个艳阳高照的夏日午后，再也没有比在一片荒地上挥着板球拍打板球奔跑嬉戏更好玩的了。据他们说，他们玩的板球游戏是世界上最棒的运动。

他的哥哥昌杜拿下了 6 分，球正好飞到了荆棘灌木层的另一侧。如果球飞出场地，保龄球队的队员应该轮流去捡球的，所以大家一致同

意轮番着去捡球,现在轮到安基斯了。但安基斯一英寸都没挪动,他在犹豫,不敢去灌木丛。安基斯的奶奶一直警告他不要去灌木丛,那是有充分理由的。棘刺锐利无比,还有一些隐藏在这片植被下的植物是有毒的,村民们曾起过严重的疹子和其他皮肤问题。但安基斯太小,还不能完全明白。

"那些灌木里寄居着最邪恶的鬼魂和其他黑暗生物。"奶奶常常这么说,甚至还讲过几个在灌木丛出没的阴险鬼魂的睡前故事。有好多次,其中的故事非但没能有助于安基斯入睡,反而让他辗转反侧,难以入睡。但这次可没那么容易逃避灌木丛,尤其是昌杜和他的小伙伴们都在的时候。昌杜对他一直很刻薄,安基斯知道昌杜和他的朋友们会抓住任何机会取笑他。直到现在,他还因为六年前,也就是七岁尿床的那件事被大家嘲笑。大家一直笑他是那么天真、好骗,奶奶说什么就信什么。安基斯不敢想象如果他不去捡球会引来怎样的冷嘲热讽。

"安基斯!你到底去不去?!"昌杜扯着嗓子喊道,邪魅地一笑。安基斯努力地想了一会儿,内心忐忑。与其一辈子被称为胆小鬼,还不如直面作祟的鬼魂,于是他下定了决心。

鬼魂和恶魔是黑暗中的生物,不是吗?他们不会在大白天出来,安基斯心里暗想,勇敢地前进。他走进灌木丛,走得越深,灌木也变得越来越细。地面是斜的,安基斯猜测球一定是滚到了边上。灌木丛生的尽头是一处悬崖,悬崖下面是幽深的山谷。安基斯慢慢地走向悬崖边缘,每走一步都小心翼翼。他一直恐高。

然而,与他马上要看到的悬崖下的会吓得他魂飞魄散的东西相比,恐高(实在)不能算是什么愚蠢的借口了。

安基斯趴在悬崖边往下看,简直不敢相信自己的眼睛。他看见了一个男人的轮廓,一个半透明的身体,摸着一块触摸不到的石头。安基斯记得自己失声尖叫,头伸了出去,身体失去平衡,栽下了悬崖。但是他究竟怎么变成现在这个样子,不管他现在是什么的样子,什么都记不起来了。安基斯升到空中,在他的身体上方盘旋。他不知道自己是怎么做到的,或者还能做什么。但他必须找到解决办法,这真是太不正常了。

"不好意思吓着你了,孩子。"安基斯听到后面有声音。他急转身往后看,原来是刚才看到的那个半透明的男人。安基斯只能从他半透明的脸上的皱纹看出他是个老人,而他身体的其他部位像他的头发一样是白的。他似乎能发出微弱的光来。安基斯急忙后退了几步,穿过一棵桃树。

"你不用怕我,也不用怕自己,孩子。不要害怕……"老人的鬼魂安慰道,试图让安基斯冷静下来。

"你的球在那儿,树后面……"他指着旁边的一棵桃树说道。"你是——你是——你是个——"安基斯结结巴巴地说。

老人轻声笑了笑,用尴尬的语气来回答这个问题,因为这个问题以前从来没有人问起。

"嗯……从最简单的意义上来讲,是的,我是。"他说道。

安基斯不由得心潮起伏。刚才短短的时间里他见证了最神奇的事情。他不敢相信自己站在那里和一个鬼魂说话。奶奶说的都是真的,好吧,至少大部分是真的。老人面相慈祥,举止随和。他没有露出恶相或吓人,除了一点——就像他说的那样"从最简单的意义上来讲,是个鬼"。

"你还有同伴吗?"安基斯好奇地问。

"当然。他们回家了,在神庙旁边的墓地里。你知道的,他们不喜欢暴露在日光下。他们说太阳会淡化他们的光泽。我只是恰巧在这里——呃——呃——"他说着，看了会儿身后的悬崖，又转身面对着安基斯，简略地把句子说完，"办点私事。"

"我也死了吗？我也是鬼吗？"安基斯忧心忡忡地问。

"呃……我不这么认为……"老人鬼魂说道，面孔扭曲，若有所思。

"那我是什么？"安基斯问。老人露出另一副若有所思的面孔。

"嗯，你看，孩子，鬼只是对曾经真实存在过的事物的印象……如果愿意，你可以把我们视为一种回忆，或者一张相片，唯一不一样的是我们可以动，能走能说话。"老人给安基斯解释道。安基斯全神贯注地听着，毕竟没有多少人可以得到聆听鬼魂说教的机会。

"我们是对曾经真实存在过的事物的反映，所以我们有确定的形态……无形但确定。但是孩子，你是没有形态的。如果我猜得没错，你的意外投射导致灵魂出窍，我可以相当肯定这是因为刚才吓得失足从悬崖栽下导致的。但是你确实做了。"

"这么说我还活着？"安基斯兴奋地问。想到有希望复生让他欣喜若狂。

"是的，我亲爱的孩子……用医生的话说，你还在昏迷中。你可以随时选择醒过来。"老人的鬼魂饶有智慧地说道。

"意外投射，灵魂出窍……嗯。"安基斯在脑海中重复着这句话。他甚至不知道是什么意思，但是听到自己还能复活还是感到很高兴。

"所以——所以我必须回到我的身体里……"安基斯努力思考着。这时，他听到昌杜和他的朋友们在尖声喊着他的名字。他进入灌木丛已经好几分钟了，他们是来找他的，或者说按照哥哥的性格，也许只是来找球的。突然，安基斯脑海里闪过一个想法。

"能帮我个忙吗？"安基斯柔声问道。

"说吧!我的孩子。"

"可以吓吓我的哥哥和他的朋友吗?他们总是对我很刻薄。"安基斯问。老人听到这个孩子气的请求,不禁哈哈大笑起来。

"你是知道的,孩子,"他边轻声笑着边说,笑得根本停不下来,"虽然听起来不怎么道德,但我没办法拒绝这么可爱的要求。毕竟我是个鬼,最好还是像鬼一点好。"说罢,他行云流水般从安基斯身旁猛扑下来,滑过悬崖。安基斯也迅速升起,他不想错过一生都值得珍惜的场景。

他看见老人追着哥哥和他的朋友们跑,伸出舌头,发出咕噜咕噜的声音。昌杜见到这骇人的鬼,飞奔逃命,尖叫着,踩在朋友们的身上,其中几个朋友绊倒了,跌在有毒的灌木丛上。安基斯想,这下大家要过很长时间才能重新开始玩板球了,如果他们还敢回来的话。

老人回来了,被自己的表演逗笑了,两个人都前仰后合笑得肚子疼,忘了在目前的状态下两人谁都没有肚子。

"所以……是时候说再见了。"安基斯缓慢而沉痛地说道,意识到不得不忍痛分别。

"你会再来看我的,对吧?我会介绍我的朋友给你认识,都是好伙计,当然都是死人……但是人很好。"老人说道。

"当然!!我每天都要来看您!"安基斯兴高采烈地说。

"孩子,我也想请你帮个忙。"

"说吧!"安基斯模仿老人的口气说道,得意地、开玩笑地轻声笑着。"你能在悬崖下的那块岩石上刻上我的名字吗?会很好看,你觉得呢?我已经试了好几天,但你知道,做鬼是有不便之处的。"他的声音变得低沉。他身体向下,从地面上抓起一块石头,但手穿过那块石头却握不住,石头还在那里原地不动。

安基斯非常乐意帮这个忙,他告别了老人,回到了自己的身体里。他捡起一块石头马上开始刻印,用一种老人喜欢的方式刻出了老人的名字。他的这段一生中难得的经历(回想起来,这话听着有点讽刺意味),只是接下来的那几年里他最愉快暑假的开端。

Astral Ankith

By Gotham Ganesh, Ashwand Srihanland

It had been a few minutes since he had died, if one could call it that. Ankith sat beside himself, looking at his stale motionless body, a feeling of numbness engulfing him. He felt like a million thoughts crossed his mind and no thoughts at all, at the same time. He wondered if he could still call it his mind; he was after all, in layman's term, a ghost.

Ankith looked down upon himself. He wasn't even sure if he was a ghost. He had no form, not even an outline. He could not see himself. He was not even sure how he was able to see, for he had no eyes. All he felt was a sense of his own presence, the knowledge of his manifestation. But the man…that man beneath the cliff…Ankith had seen him, his translucent figure…Could he have been…Was it possible? Ankith wondered in bewilderment.

Ankith could remember pristinely how it had happened. He remembered playing cricket with his brother and his friends. It was the summer holidays and how better to entertain oneself than by frolicking around a barren ground with a bat and a ball on a hot sunny afternoon. They were playing cricket which according to them was the best game in the world.

His elder brother Chandru scored 6 points and the ball just flew to the other side of the thorn bushes. It had been agreed that the bowling team members would take turns in fetching the ball if it went off the ground and it was Ankith's turn to fetch the ball now. But Ankith barely moved an inch, hesitating to go into the bushes. Ankith's Grandma had always warned him against going into the bushes and for good reason. The thorns were razor sharp and some of the plants that the patchy vegetation housed were poisonous and had caused severe rashes and other skin disorders to the villagers. But Ankith was too young to understand all that.

"The bushes are home to the meanest ghosts and other dark creatures," his Grandma would say. She had even spun several bedtime tales of the treacherous ghosts that haunted the bushes, most of which left Ankith sleepless on many occasions instead of lulling him to sleep. But ducking the bushes would not be possible this time, not with Chandru and his gang around. Chandru had always been mean to him, and Ankith knew he would gang up with his friends and tease him at the slightest chance he gets. After all, he was still being teased for the bed wetting incident that happened when he was seven, and that was six years ago. He had always been mocked for being so naive and gullible and believing everything that Grandma said. Ankith dreaded to think of all the taunts he would receive if he refused to go.

"Ankith! Are you going or what?!" Chandru shouted from the pitch, with an evil grin on his face. Ankith thought hard for a few jittery moments. It was better to face haunting ghosts than to be called a coward for the rest of his life, he decided.

The ghosts and monsters are the creatures of the dark, aren't they? They wouldn't come out by day, he said to himself and braved forward. Ankith walked into the bushes, past the shrubs which seemed to be thinning as he went further down. The ground was sloping and Ankith figured that the ball must have rolled down to the edge. The bushy terrain gave way to a cliff beneath which was a deep trough. Ankith trailed towards the edge of the cliff, warily inching forward, looking for the ball. He had always been scared of heights.

But then, what he was going to see beneath the cliff was about to scare the life out of him(literally) so much that his fear of heights seemed too silly a reason to be afraid.

When Ankith leaned over to see beyond the cliff, he couldn't believe his eyes. What he saw was the outline of a man, a translucent figure, fiddling with a stone he was unable to grope. Ankith remembered screaming his head out, losing his balance and toppling down the cliff. But how he had become what he was, whatever he was, he had no recollection. Ankith rose up into the air, hovering slightly above his body. He did not know how he could do that, or what else he could do. But he had to find a way to fix it. This was not normal.

"I'm sorry for giving you a scare there, son," he heard a voice behind him. Ankith shifted his view abruptly to look behind him. It was the translucent man from before. He looked old, but Ankith could tell that only from the wrinkles on his translucent face, for the rest of his body was as white as his hair. He seemed to be dimly glowing. Ankith retracted a few steps hastily, gliding through a peach tree as he went.

"You have as little to fear me as you have to fear yourself, son. Don't be afraid…" the old man's ghost said soothingly, trying to calm Ankith.

"And your ball is there, behind that tree…" he said pointing to an adjacent peach tree. "Are you—Are you—Are you a—" Ankith stuttered.

The old man gave a chuckle and answered in an embarrassed tone, as he had never been asked that question before.

"Hmmm…In the simplest sense of it, yes I am," he said.

Ankith's mind stirred. He had witnessed the most bizarre things in a few short moments. He couldn't believe he was standing there, making conversation with a ghost. His grandma had been right, well at least for most parts of it. The old man had a kind face and a gregarious demeanour. Nothing about him seemed mean or scary, except for the fact that he was, as he put it— "in the simplest of terms, a ghost".

"Are there more of you?" Ankith asked curiously.

"Sure, of course. They are back home, in the graveyard by the shrine. You see they don't take a shine to the sun. They say it dulls their gleam. I just happened to be here on a—umm—uhhh—" he said looking back at the cliff for a moment. He pulled himself back to face Ankith, only to finish his sentence curtly, "on a personal chore."

"Am I dead too? Am I a ghost?" asked Ankith apprehensively.

"Well…" the old man's ghost said, contorting his face thoughtfully, "I don't think so…"

"Then what am I ?" he questioned. The old man gave another one of his seemingly thoughtful looks.

"Well you see, son. Ghosts are just an impression of what was once real…Think of us to be a memory, or a photograph if you will, except that we can move and walk and talk," the old man explained to Ankith. Ankith listened raptly, for not many get a chance to be lectured by a ghost.

"We are a reflection of what was once real. So we have definite form…immaterial but definite. But you son, you are formless. If I'm right I think you have managed to astrally project yourself, accidentally of course, which I quite surely attribute to the shock from the fall. But still you have managed."

"So I can be alive?" Ankith asked excitedly. The prospect of getting to be alive again seemed to bring immense joy to him.

"You are, my dear boy. You are, as the doctors would put it—in a state of coma. You can just as easily choose to wake up from it," the old man's ghost said wisely.

"Astrally projected myself…hmmm," Ankith repeated in his mind. He did not even know what it meant, but he was glad to hear that he could go back.

"So—so I just have to go back to my body…" Ankith said thinking hard. Just then, Ankith heard screams of Chandru and his friends shouting his name. It had been more than a few minutes since he had wandered into the bushes and they had come in search of him, or knowing his brother, maybe just in search of the ball. Suddenly, an idea struck him.

"Could I ask you something?" Ankith said tenderly.

"Ask away, my son."

"Could you scare my brother and his friends for me? They are always mean to me," he asked. The old man laughed hard at the childish plea.

"You know, son," he said still chuckling, unable to subside his laughter, "As immoral as it sounds, I stand unable to say no to such a cute request. I am a ghost after all, I might as well behave like one," he said and swooped across Ankith in one fluid motion and glided over the cliff. Ankith rose above quickly as he did not want to miss the scene that he was going to cherish for the rest of his life.

He saw the old man chasing his brother and his friends, waggling his tongue and grunting. Chandru ran for his life, screaming at the frightening sight, trampling over his friends, some of who tripped and fell over the poisonous shrubs. It would be a long time before any of them would be able to play cricket, Ankith thought; that is if they ever dared to come back.

The old man came back, amused at his own performance and they both shared a rib cracking laugh, overlooking the fact that neither of them had any ribs in their present state.

"So…I think it is time to say goodbye then," Ankith said heavily, the realization of having to depart befell him.

"You will visit me again won't you? I'll introduce you to my friends, good chaps they are. Dead of course…but good," he said.

"Of course!! I'm going to visit every day!" Ankith replied, elatedly.

"And I have a small favour to ask of you too, son."

"Ask away…" Ankith said imitating the old man, chortling kiddingly while doing so. "Could you etch my name on that rock under the cliff…It would look good don't you think… I have been trying for days, but you know, being a ghost has its disadvantages." he said, his voice dipping in tone. He moved down to grab a stone from the ground but his hand just went through the stone unable to disturb it and the stone just lay there unaffected.

Ankith was only too happy to agree and he bid his goodbye and returned to his body. He picked up a stone and got to work at once, carving out the old man's name in a fashion that pleased him. He had had the experience of a lifetime (how ironic that sounds in retrospect) and it was just the beginning of what was going to be his best summer holiday for years to come.

玫瑰的玫瑰

红玫瑰花是她的最爱,她名字也叫玫瑰。每年她的丈夫都要送她打着漂亮蝴蝶结的红玫瑰。那年他去世以后的情人节,还有玫瑰花送到了她的门口,卡片上写着:"我的情人节礼物",跟往年一样。

每年他送她红玫瑰,卡片上总这样说:"我今年更爱你,比去年的今天更爱。""岁月流转又一年,我对你的爱增长在每一天。"她知道这会是玫瑰花最后一次出现了。她想,他是提前订了玫瑰花。她亲爱的丈夫不知道,他即将不久于人世。他总喜欢提前做好准备,这样,如果到时候他很忙的话,每件事都照样运转,妥帖停当。她修剪好花茎,把它们插进一个特别的花瓶里,然后,将花瓶放在他满脸笑容的照片旁,她会在她丈夫喜欢的椅子上坐上好几个小时,看着他的照片,玫瑰就放在那里。

时间过了一年,她失去了伴侣的日子好难挨。孤单寂寞冷,渐渐成了她的命。然而,就在那个时间,跟以往情人节送花的时间一样,门铃响了,玫瑰花到了。她将玫瑰拿进屋,目瞪口呆地看着。然后,她拿起电话打给花店。接电话的是花店店主,她问店主能否解释一下,为什么有人要给她送花,勾起她的伤心往事?

"我知道,你的丈夫一年多前去世了,"店主说,"我知道你会打电话来的,你想知道是怎么回事。""今天你收到的花,已经提前付了钱。""你的丈夫总是提前计划,他做事绝不靠碰运气。"

"这里有一份委托书,我已存档。他预付了花款,委托我们每年给你送花。嗯,你每年都会在情人节前夕收到玫瑰花。还有另外一件事,我想应该告诉你,他还写了一张特别的小卡片……他几年前就写好了的。"

"这样,如果我发现他已不在人世的话,就把这张卡片……这张卡片在接下来的那年寄给你。"

她谢了他,挂了电话,不禁泪如雨下。她慢慢地伸手去拿卡片,手指在颤抖。在卡片里,她看到了他写给她的短笺。她屏息静气地读着,默默无语。他是这样写的:"亲爱的,我知道,我离开你已经一年了,但愿你这段日子不要太难挨。""我知道,你一定很孤单,这种痛苦确实是刻骨铭心的。因为如果换成我,我也会有同样的感受。我们之间的爱让生命中的点点滴滴都是那么美好,语言是乏力的,我对你的爱无法表达,你是我完美的贤妻。"

"你还是我的挚友和爱人,你满足了我对妻子的所有想象。我知道,这才过了一年,但我还是要你努力节哀顺变。我想让你快乐,即便流泪也是快乐的泪水,所以我要继续送你玫瑰花,一年不落。"

"当你收到这些玫瑰花时,想想我们一起度过的快乐时光,我们曾经是多么幸福呀!我一直深爱着你,我也知道,我的爱没有止境。但是,亲爱的,答应我,一定要好好活着,来日方长。"

"请你努力寻找快乐,度过余生。我知道,这谈何容易?但我仍希望你想方设法去做。玫瑰花每年都会如期而至,除非你不再听到敲门声出来,花店不会停止送玫瑰花。"

"每年情人节前夕,花店会派人来送五次花,以防你外出不在家。五次来访都寻人不见以后,送花人便可确定把玫瑰花送到我告诉他们的另一个地方,送到我们所在的地方,那就是我们的重逢之地。"

Roses for Rose

Red roses were her favorites, her name was also Rose. And every year her husband sent them, tied with pretty bows. The year he died, the roses were delivered to her door. The card said, "Be my Valentine", like all the years before.

Each year he sent her roses, and the note would always say, "I love you even more this year, than last year on this day." "My love for you will always grow, with every passing year." She knew this was the last time that the roses would appear. She thought, he ordered roses in advance before this day. Her loving husband did not know, that he would pass away. He always liked to do things early. Then, if he got too busy, everything would work out fine. She trimmed the stems, and placed them in a very special vase. Then, sat the vase beside the portrait of his smiling face. She would sit for hours, in her husband's favorite chair. While staring at his picture, and the roses sitting there.

A year went by, and it was hard to live without her mate. With loneliness and solitude, that had become her fate. Then, the very hour, as on Valentines before, the door-bell rang, and there were roses, sitting by her door. She brought the roses in, and then just looked at them in shock. Then, went to get the telephone, to call the florist shop. The owner answered, and she asked him, if he would explain, why would someone do this to her, causing her such pain?

"I know your husband passed away, more than a year ago," The owner said, "I knew you'd call, and you would want to know." "The flowers you received today, were paid for in advance." "Your husband always planned ahead, he left nothing to chance."

"There is a standing order, that I have on file down here. And he has paid, well in advance, you'll get them every year. There also is another thing, that I think you should know. He wrote a special little card...he did this years ago."

"Then, should ever, I find out that he's no longer here. That's the card...that should be sent, to you the following year."

She thanked him and hung up the phone, her tears now flowing hard. Her fingers shaking, as she slowly reached to get the card. Inside the card, she saw that he had written her a note. Then, as she stared in total silence, this is what he wrote: "Hello my love, I know it's been a year since I've been gone, I hope it hasn't been too hard for you to overcome." "I know it must be lonely, and the pain is very real. For if it was the other way, I know how I would feel. The love we shared made everything so beautiful in life. I loved you more than words can say, you were the perfect wife."

"You were my friend and lover, you fulfilled my every need. I know it's only been a year, but please try not to grieve. I want you to be happy, even when you shed your tears. That is why the roses will be sent to you for years."

"When you get these roses, think of all the happiness that we had together, and how both of us were blessed. I have always loved you and I know I always will. But, my love, you must go on, you have some living still."

"Please…try to find happiness, while living out your days. I know it is not easy, but I hope you find some ways. The roses will come every year, and they will only stop when your door's not answered, when the florist stops to knock."

"He will come five times that day, in case you have gone out. But after his last visit, he will know without a doubt. To take the roses to the place, where I've instructed him, and place the rose where we are, together once again."

那只最后的蝴蝶

[美国] 迈克尔·韦尔岑巴赫

我 11 岁那年,家里正准备搬家,离开我们居住了四年的美丽的日本冲绳岛。不久,我们会回到北美,然后从那里启程前往英国:我爸爸又调动工作了。

但是,对于这种不安定的漂泊生活,在我心里早已竖立起了一堵墙。我痴迷于大自然,不论我搬到哪个国家,对于大自然的痴迷都会带给我无穷无尽的欢娱和惊喜。从记事起,我就一直在收集贝壳和化石,徒步旅行,观察鸟类。当我到达这个位于太平洋上的小岛之后,我发现蝴蝶的种类多得令人吃惊,于是我开始收集蝴蝶。

迄今为止,我已经有几个装着漂亮标本的玻璃盘了,这些标本我都仔细地固定在标本架上,贴上了标签。它们大小不一,颜色各异,从深蓝、亮黄、猩红到闪亮的翠绿,不一而足。捕捉蝴蝶并非易事,所以我为自己的收集而自豪。

但是至今还有一种蝴蝶我从来没有捉到过——那就是硕大瑰丽的橙色尖翅粉蝶。去年圣诞节,我的教父送我一本精彩的、关于亚热带蝴蝶的书。其中有一页以全插图的形式,详尽地介绍了这种白色的橙色尖翅粉蝶,其蝶翼长 7 到 10 厘米,是冲绳岛最大的白蝴蝶。我不禁心驰神迷——下定决心要捉一只回来。

问题是这种蝴蝶有栖息在高处的生活习性：我只能眼巴巴地看着这些美丽的昆虫随着轻柔的海风蹁跹，在掩映着小岛中心的树梢上飞舞。无论我爬得多高，由于随身携带的捕蝶网和集蝶罐的限制，我总是够不着这些蝴蝶——它们就像树梢上橙白相间的纸屑一样。

那年夏天，所有的袋子和箱子都打了包准备启程，家里的所有东西都成了行李，我们的房间也变得空空荡荡的了。但我没让包装工人把我的捕蝶网打包，大部分时间里我都是在户外竹林间徜徉徘徊。

学校正在放暑假，再有几天我们也要离开了，我开始对找到硕大的橙色尖翅粉蝶不抱希望。一天早晨，妈妈对我说我的收集板和书籍在下午之前都必须打包装好。于是，我离开家在灌木丛和一排排的树篱间徘徊，机警地搜寻着我那可遇不可求的大美蝴蝶。

夏日炎炎，蝉儿高叫；烈日下的人行道上，有绿色的蜥蜴舞动。甘蔗林在风中轻轻泛起阵阵涟漪，山坡上，各种各样的蝴蝶要么轻巧地在野花丛上飞舞，要么机灵地躲闪在野花丛间。但是那天，硕大瑰丽的橙色尖翅粉蝶还是像往常一样，蹁跹在高高的树顶之上。最后一次捕捉仍然没有结果，我拖着身体愁眉苦脸地往家走去。

然而，当我拐过我家巷子的弯时，在生机盎然的木槿树篱旁边，瞥到一抹亮白。我抬头一看，在一米之外的地方，硕大瑰丽的橙色尖翅粉蝶正趴在一朵巨大的猩红色花朵上。它在吸食花蜜，翅翼颤动着，我顿时动弹不得，呆若木鸡。过了好长一会儿，我才开始慢慢地举起捕蝶网，一点一点地靠近它，我的心怦怦直跳，汗水顺着眉毛缓缓地流了下来。

突然，这只大美蝴蝶飞了起来，转移到了另一朵花上。我纵身一跃。最终，我梦寐以求的宝物到手了，它在我精密的捕蝶网中奋力扑打着翅膀。我简直不敢相信自己的眼睛，不敢相信自己有这么好的运气。

我轻轻地伸出手，抓住了那只蝴蝶的胸部，十分想把它扔进灭蝶罐中，那样，罐中致命的甲醛马上就会起作用。但当我的手伸向罐子时，又突然愣住了，我惊异地注视着另一只手中那梦寐以求的大美蝴蝶，蝴蝶生机勃勃的白色双翼顶端点缀着如彩虹般绚丽的橙色花纹，我能感受到指间这只小生命的惊惧，它的小腿在我的掌间疯狂地蹬着。

那时，我突然心血来潮，将自己长期以来苦苦追寻的战利品抛向了清澈晴朗的天空，看着它像完美生动的千纸鹤一样远走高飞了。大美蝴蝶在旁边的树木上空掠过，接着在我的视野中消失了。

两天后，我也飞离了这个绿色的小岛，去往一个未知的家。在这座岛屿的某处，我的大美蝴蝶蹁跹在树丛的上空，那么遥不可及，我只拥有了一瞬间。

爱也是这样。

The Last Butterfly

By Micheal Welzenbach

I was 11, and my family was preparing to leave the beautiful Japanese island of Okinawa, where we had lived for four years. Shortly we'd head back to North America, thence to England: My father was being transferred yet again.

But I had constructed a mental wall against this unsettledness. My fascination with nature, in whatever country I moved to, provided me with an endless source of distraction and amazement. I'd been collecting seashells and fossils, hiking and bird-watching since I could remember. And when I had arrived on this little island in the Pacific Ocean, I discovered a startling variety of butterflies, and I began to collect them.

By now I had several glass-topped trays of glorious specimens, carefully labeled and mounted. They came in all sizes and hues, from deepest blues to brilliant yellows, scarlets and shimmering emerald greens. Catching butterflies wasn't easy, so I was proud of my collection.

But there was one that I had yet to capture—the magnificent great orange tip. The previous Christmas I had received from my godfather a marvelous book on subtropical butterflies. It included a fully illustrated page with scientific information on this orange-tipped white that, with its seven to ten-centimetre wingspan, was Okinawa's largest white. I was entranced—and determined to have one.

The problem was its lofty habitat: I could only watch these lovely insects floating gracefully on the sea breeze, high above the canopy of trees that shrouded the centre of the island. No matter how high I climbed, encumbered by my net and collection jars, these creatures were always just beyond my reach—like white and orange confetti settled on the treetops.

As the bags and boxes were packed that summer for our departure, the household was steadily converted into luggage, and our bungalow rang hollow. Yet I kept my butterfly net clear of the packers' hands and spent most of my time outdoors, ranging through the bamboo.

With school out for the summer and only a couple of days before we were to leave, I began to give up hope of finding my great orange tip. My mother told me one morning that my collection panels and books had to be packed up by afternoon Meanwhile I was at leave to wander the bush and the hedgerows, keeping a wary eye out for my elusive beauty.

In the dense heat, the cicadas buzzed and green lizards danced on the sidewalks in the burning sun. The seas of sugarcane rippled gently in the air, and butterflies of all sorts floated or dodged briskly above the wildflowers on the hillsides. But as usual, the great orange tips remained high above the treetops that day. I traipsed home disconsolately after my fruitless, final search.

But then, as I rounded the corner of our culdesac, alongside the vibrant hibiscus hedge, I caught a flash of brilliant white out of the corner of my eye. I looked up and there it was, about a metre away, settled on one of the big scarlet flowers. As it fed on the nectar, its wings moved tremulously and I froze in my tracks, transfixed. After a long moment, I began to raise my net, little by little, my heart pounding, the sweat trickling down my brow.

Suddenly the big beauty was aloft, moving to another flower. I swung. And there at last was the coveted prize, beating furiously in the fine mesh of my trap. I could scarcely believe my eyes or my luck.

Gently I reached in and grabbed the butterfly by the thorax, with every intention of nudging it into the killing jar, where the deadly formaldehyde would quickly do its work. But my hand froze as I reached for the jar, and I simply gazed, astonished, at the grail in my other hand. There was the brilliant, iridescent bloom of orange on the tips of its glowing white wings, and I could feel the creature's fear between my fingers. Its little legs scrambled frantically in my palm.

And then, on an impulse, I tossed my long-sought prize into the clear, bright air and watched it float away like a perfect, living origami. High above the nearby trees it sailed, then disappeared from sight.

Two days later I, too, was soaring over the little green island, headed for a home I didn't know. My butterfly was down there somewhere, hovering above the trees, distant and only fleetingly attainable.

Love is like that.

儿子理发

[英国]肯·埃尔克斯

大卫走出前门时,一道白色的炽热阳光瞬间照得他眼睛花了,他本能地抓住了爸爸的手。

这是今年第一个真正暖起来的日子,春夏之交的热度让人出乎意料。父亲和儿子正走在去理发店的路上,这是他们经常一起做的事情。

一直都是这样的,路线都是一样的。"是时候修理修理你那乱蓬蓬的头发啦。"大卫的爸爸用夹着香烟的两根指头指着他说。"也许我该给你剪。大剪刀在哪儿呢,珍妮特?"

有时,爸爸会在客厅里追他,假装要剪掉他的耳朵。小的时候,大卫一紧张就哭,害怕真的失去他的耳朵,但他已经长大了,早已经明白了。

塞缪尔斯先生的理发店是一个长形的房间,在薯条店上面,要上一截很陡的楼梯才能到。每一个台阶上都有磨损的沟槽,是那些上上下下、川流不息的人们留下的。大卫跟着父亲,他有些恼怒,为他不能像父亲那样每上一个台阶就发出嘎吱嘎吱的响声而烦恼。

大卫喜欢这家理发店,这家店不像他去过的其他地方。这里混杂着烟味、男人味和发油的味道。有时候,门开的时候,薯条的味道会和爬楼梯的顾客一起上来，等候理发的人们会一起抬起头来吸吸鼻子。

屋子的最里面挂满了黑白照片，照片里的人梳着各种各样的过气的发型，在那儿的地板上有两把固定的理发椅。理发椅也过气了，非常笨重，配有脚踏打气泵。每当塞缪尔斯先生调整座位高度的时候，脚踏泵都会发出嘶嘶、吱吱的声音，他脖子上的肉也微微地皱在一起。

椅子前面是带淋浴头的洗脸池，长长的金属软管接在水龙头上，看起来没有人使用。洗脸池后面挂着镜子，洗脸池的两边都是架子，架子上堆满了塑料梳子和其他东西，其他东西包括一些盛满了蓝色液体的玻璃碗，剃须杯、剪刀、剃须刀、梳子，整齐地堆放着，呈金字塔状，还有10罐鲜红色的百利发乳。

屋子后面坐着顾客们，大多数时候店里都静悄悄的，除了塞缪尔斯先生暂停理发吸一口烟，吐出来的灰蓝色烟像是风筝尾巴似的扭动着飘入空气中。

轮到大卫理发了，塞缪尔斯先生给椅子扶手上搭了一块木板，上面还盖着一张牛血红皮革，这样的话他就不用弯腰给小孩理发了。大卫爬上了这个临时搭成的长凳。

"就你个子窜的这个速度，很快就用不着这个了，到时候就能坐椅子上了。"塞缪尔斯先生说道。

"哇哦。"大卫说，扭过身去看他爸爸，忘了自己完全可以在镜子里看到他。"爸爸，塞缪尔斯先生说我很快就能坐椅子里，不用这块板了！"

"我听到了。"他父亲回应道，眼睛没抬，还在看报纸。"我猜到了那个时候塞缪尔斯先生给你理发就会涨价了。"

"至少双倍的价格。"塞缪尔斯先生说，朝大卫眨眨眼。

最后，大卫的爸爸从报纸上抬起头，往镜子里扫了一眼，看见他的儿子正看着他。他笑了。

"不久前我还得把你抱上那块木板,那个时候你自己还爬不上去呢。"他父亲说道。

"小孩子,不会永远小的。"塞缪尔斯先生说道。店里所有人都点头表示同意。大卫也跟着点了点头。

在镜子里,他看见塞缪尔斯先生给他围了一件长长的尼龙斗篷,他小小的头从里面钻出来,塞缪尔斯先生绕着衣领给他塞了一块楔形的棉絮。时不时地,他偷偷看看给他剪头发的理发师。当理发师围着他来回走动的时候,他闻到了一股难闻的汗味和须后水混合的味道,塞缪尔斯先生一边梳一边剪,一边剪一边梳。

大卫觉得自己仿佛置身于另外一个世界,除了理发师在油地毡上拖着脚走路的声音和剪刀的咔嚓声,周围静悄悄的。在窗户的反射中,他能看到窗外的东西,几片云彩缓缓地穿过窗框,随剪刀的咔嚓声飘着。

他睡眼惺忪的目光落到斗篷的前面,他的头发像雪花似的轻柔地飘落,他想象着自己跟那些男人和大男孩一样坐在椅子上,特殊长椅靠着墙,在那个角落里。

他想起了姨妈圣诞节送他的圣经故事图画书,其中有一张是黛利拉剪了参孙的头发。大卫想知道他的力气会不会和参孙一样,一剪就没了。

塞缪尔斯先生理完了,大卫从座位上跳了下来,把脸上令人发痒的碎头发擦掉。他低头一看,自己浓密的金发和前面那些顾客棕色、灰色、黑色的头发散落在地上。有那么一瞬间,他想弯腰把自己剪下来的金发跟那些头发分开并且捡起来,但已经来不及了。

等他们走出理发店来到人行道上的时候,阳光还是很强烈,却不那么毒了,太阳已经快要落山了。

"要不这样吧,小伙子,咱们买点炸鱼和薯条带回家吧,你妈妈也就不用煮茶了。"大卫的爸爸说道,两人走在街道上。

小伙子很激动,拉着爸爸的手。厚厚的手温柔而又紧紧握着他的手,大卫惊讶地发现,爸爸温暖的掌心里握着他的一缕金发。

David's Haircut

By Ken Elkes

When David steps out of the front door he is blinded for a moment by the white, fizzing sunlight and reaches instinctively for his dad's hand.

It's the first really warm day of the year, an unexpected heat that bridges the cusp between spring and summer. Father and son are on their way to the barbershop, something they have always done together.

Always, the routine is the same. "It's about time we got that mop of yours cut," David's dad will say, pointing at him with two fingers, a cigarette wedged between them. "Perhaps I should do it. Where are those shears Janet?"

Sometimes his dad chases him round the living room, pretending to cut off his ears. When he was young David used to get too excited and start crying, scared that maybe he really would lose his ears, but he has long since grown out of that.

Mr. Samuels' barbershop is in a long room above the chip

shop, reached by a steep flight of stairs. There is a groove worn in each step by the men who climb and descend in a regular stream. David follows his father, annoyed that he cannot make each step creak like his old man can.

David loves the barbershop, it's like nowhere else he goes. It smells of cigarettes and men and hair oil. Sometimes the smell of chips will climb the stairs along with a customer and when the door opens the waiting men lift their noses together.

Black and white photographs of men with various out-of-fashion hairstyles hang above a picture rail at the end of the room, where two barber's chairs are bolted to the floor. They are heavy, old-fashioned chairs with foot pumps that hiss and chatter as Mr. Samuels, the rolls of his plump neck squashing slightly, adjusts the height of the seat.

In front of the chairs are deep sinks with a showerhead and long metal hose attached to the taps, not that anyone seems to use them. Behind the sinks are mirrors and on either side of these, shelves overflowing with an mixture of plastic combs (some plunged into a glass bowl containing a blue liquid), shaving mugs, scissors, cut throat razors, hair brushes, stacked neatly in a pyramid, and 10 bright red tubs of Brylcreem.

At the back of the room sit the customers, silent for most of the time, except when Mr. Samuels breaks off from cutting and takes a drag on his cigarette, sending a wisp of grey-blue smoke like the tail of kite twisting into the air.

When it is David's turn for a cut, Mr. Samuels places a wooden board covered with a piece of oxblood red leather across the arms of the chair, so that the barber doesn't have to stoop to cut the boy's hair. David scrambles up onto the bench.

"The rate you're shooting up, you won't need this soon, you'll be sat in the chair," the barber says.

"Wow," says David, squirming round to look at his dad, forgetting that he can see him through the mirror. "Dad, Mr. Samuels said I could be sitting in the chair soon, not just on the board!"

"So I hear," his father replies, not looking up from the paper. "I expect Mr. Samuels will start charging me more for your hair then."

"At least double the price," said Mr. Samuels, winking at David.

Finally David's dad looks up from his newspaper and glances into the mirror, seeing his son looking back at him. He smiles.

"Wasn't so long ago when I had to lift you onto that board because you couldn't climb up there yourself," he says.

"They don't stay young for long do they, kids," Mr. Samuels declares. All the men in the shop nod in agreement. David nods too.

In the mirror he sees a little head sticking out of a long nylon cape that Mr. Samuels has swirled around him and folded into his collar with a wedge of cotton wool. Occasionally he steals glances at the barber as he works. He smells a mixture of stale sweat and aftershave as the barber's moves around him, combing and snipping, combing and snipping.

David feels like he is in another world, noiseless except for the scuffing of the barber's shoes on the lino and the snap of his scissors. In the reflection from the window he could see through the window, a few small clouds moved slowly through the frame, moving to the sound of the scissors' click.

Sleepily, his eyes dropping to the front of the cape where his hair falls with the same softness as snow and he imagines sitting in the chair just like the men and older boys, the special bench left leaning against the wall in the corner.

He thinks about the picture book of bible stories his aunt gave him for Christmas, the one of Samson having his hair cut by Delilah. David wonders if his strength will go like Samson's.

When Mr. Samuels has finished, David hops down from the seat, rubbing the itchy hair from his face. Looking down he sees his own thick, blonde hair scattered among the browns, greys and blacks of the men who have sat in the chair before him. For a moment he wants to reach down and gather up the broken blonde locks, to separate them from the others, but he does not have time.

The sun is still strong when they reach the pavement outside the shop, but it is less fiery now, already beginning to drop from its zenith.

"I tell you what, lad, let's get some fish and chips to take home, save your mum from cooking tea," says David's dad and turns up the street.

The youngster is excited and grabs his dad's hand. The thick-skinned fingers close gently around his and David is surprised to find, warming in his father's palm, a lock of his own hair.

叉子掉了

一岁半的伊桑和妈妈、姐姐伊莎贝尔坐在餐桌边吃午饭。伊桑用叉子叉了一大块胡萝卜放进嘴里。一边吃着,一边拿着叉子拍着桌子:"嗒嗒嗒……"

"啪!"叉子掉到了地板上。

伊桑用小手指指着地板喊道:"掉!"妈妈过去把叉子捡起,在水龙头下冲了冲,还给了伊桑。伊桑一拿回叉子,就兴奋地摇晃着双腿,欢快地对妈妈说:"谢谢!"

妈妈微笑:"不用谢。"妈妈回应了一个微笑。伊桑又像刚才那样拿着叉子玩了起来。

"啪!"叉子又掉地板上了,伊桑又喊道:"掉!掉!"

妈妈又捡起叉子还给了伊桑,他又向她道了谢。

叉子第三次掉到了地上。伊莎贝尔看着弟弟咯咯地笑。妈妈警告说:"不许再扔了! 再扔不让你用它吃饭了。"叉子又重回到伊桑手里。

"啪!啪!"小家伙这次拿起了勺子和叉子一齐扔在了地上,面无表情地说:"掉!掉!"

妈妈生气地看着他,一动不动。

伊莎贝尔飞快地从桌子前站了起来,捡起叉子和勺子,拿到水龙头下面冲了冲,把它们放回到伊桑的餐垫上。

伊莎贝尔回到自己的座位坐下。姐弟俩相视而笑，伊桑心满意足地说："谢谢！"

伊莎贝尔也心满意足地回答："不用谢！"

妈妈说："你俩都好好吃饭。不许再扔餐具了！伊桑再扔，伊莎贝尔也不许捡……"

妈妈的话音未落，小家伙已经把勺子又扔到了地板上去了，还看着伊莎贝尔："掉！掉！"

妈妈一回头，发现伊莎贝尔已经消失在桌子底下。

伊莎贝尔把叉子从桌子下放回伊桑的手里，又从桌子底下偷偷把勺子放回到他的餐垫上。

伊莎贝尔回自己的座位上。伊桑是那么开心，他真诚地对伊莎贝尔说："谢谢。"

妈妈严肃地看着伊桑说："伊桑，如果你再扔两次的话，我就不让你坐在这里吃饭了。你就到姐姐房间去静一静。"妈妈指了指伊莎贝尔的卧室。

但是伊桑好像没听见似的，把勺子扔到了地板上，对着伊莎贝尔喊道："掉！掉！"

伊莎贝尔马上又潜到了桌子底下。

妈妈默默地看他们接着玩了两轮扔与捡的游戏。然后，她站起身，把伊桑从座位里拎了出来，抱到伊莎贝尔的卧室里去。"现在不许你吃饭了。"她说着就把伊桑放下了。伊桑还没回过神来，妈妈已经把门在他面前关上了。

伊桑立刻放声大哭了起来。以他的身高，还不足以够到门把手拧开门。他碰到了门把手，门把手动了动，却没打开。他哭个不停。

在餐桌上，伊莎贝尔用手掌拍着桌子，生气地对着妈妈说："他只是个小孩！如果你不马上把他放出来，我今天就不听你的话了！"妈妈装作没听见伊莎贝尔说的话，静静地吃饭。但是，她还是竖起耳朵听着伊桑的哭声。伊桑的哭声有节奏，有力量，不用担心背过气去。

妈妈心里好奇：平时小家伙最喜欢钻到姐姐的卧室里去，在每个角落都能发现好玩的东西。现在一个人被反锁在里面，怎么哭得这么厉害？看来他明白这是惩罚。

小家伙在屋里哭了两分钟，并没有不哭或者缓解的意思。妈妈开始有点担心。

伊莎贝尔已经出离愤怒了："快把他放出来，现在！马上！如果你现在不把他放出来，我就去把他放出来！"妈妈看了她一眼，起身去给可怜的小家伙开门。

一打开门，伊桑就止住了哭声。他扑到妈妈的怀里来，两个胳膊紧紧搂着妈妈的脖子，小脸贴着妈妈的脸，叫了好几声妈妈。

妈妈说："如果你再把叉子、勺子扔到地板上，妈妈还是会这样把你关进姐姐的卧室里。从现在开始，不要再扔了，好吗？"伊桑说："好的。"

妈妈把他抱回餐桌他的座位上，伊桑坐下来安安静静地吃饭。就这么规规矩矩地吃了好一会儿后，姐弟俩目光相遇，两人都咧嘴大笑起来。小家伙手又痒了，忍不住又要玩那个游戏。他一把抓起勺子往餐桌上扔，看着姐姐说："哎哟……"

伊莎贝尔微微一笑，撑起身来帮他把勺子从餐桌上捡起来，放回到他的餐垫上。伊桑马上高兴地说："谢谢！"

对于这一幕，妈妈装作没看见：两个小家伙还真是好搭档，只要别扔到地板上就行。

The Fork Dropped

Ethan sat at table with Mom and Sister Isabelle for lunch. He is about 18 months old. Ethan picked up a chunk of carrot with a fork and put it into his mouth. He patted the table with the fork while chewing the carrot. "Dah-dah-dah…"

"Pah!" The fork dropped to the floor.

Ethan pointed his little finger to the floor and called: "Drop!" Mom went to pick up the fork, rinsed it under water and returned it back to Ethan. Having the fork back in his hand, Ethan dangled his legs excitedly and said to Mom gleefully: "Thanks!"

"You're welcome!" Mom responded with a smile. Ethan played the fork as before.

"Pah!" The fork dropped to the floor again. Ethan called out again: "Drop! Drop!"

Mom picked up the fork again and returned it to Ethan. Ethan thanked her again.

The fork dropped to the floor the third time. Isabelle watched at Ethan and giggled. Mom warned: "Don't throw it again! Otherwise, I won't let you eat with it." The fork went back to

Ethan's hand again.

"Pah! Pah!" This time the little guy threw both the spoon and the fork to the floor. He pointed at them and called out with a blank face: "Drop! Drop!"

Mom looked at Ethan sullenly and didn't move.

Isabelle stormed from her seat, picked up both the fork and the spoon, rinsed them under faucet, and returned both of them back to Ethan's placemat.

Isabelle went back to her seat. The sister and brother looked at each other with smile on both faces. Ethan said with satisfaction: "Thanks!"

Isabelle responded with satisfaction: "You're welcome!"

Mom said: "Both of you focus on eating. No throwing of utensils again! If Ethan throws them again, Isabelle is not allowed to pick them…"

When Mom has hardly finished her sentence, Ethan has already thrown his spoon to the floor. He watched at Isabelle: "Drop! Drop!"

Mom turned her head to discover that Isabelle has already disappeared under table.

Isabelle put the fork back into Ethan's hand under table. She then put the spoon back on his placemat from under furtively.

Isabelle went back to her seat. Ethan was so happy. He said earnestly to Isabelle: "Thanks."

Mom looked at Ethan seriously: "Ethan, if you have twice more of throwing, I won't let you sit here and eat. You will have a time-out at your sister's room." Mom pointed in the direction of Isabelle's room.

But again, as if he didn't understand Mom's words, Ethan threw the spoon to the floor and called out to Isabelle: "Drop! Drop!"

Isabelle dived under the table at once.

Mom watched them play the drop-and-pick game twice more silently. Then she stood up, lifted Ethan from the seat and took him to Isabelle's room. "Then you are not allowed to eat now." She said as she put down Ethan. Before Ethan figured it out, Mom has already closed the door in front of him.

Ethan cried out aloud instantly. He is not high enough to grab and turn the door knob. He touched the knob and move it a bit, but couldn't open it. He cried aloud constantly.

At dining table, Isabelle smacked the table with her palm and said angrily at Mom: "He is only a baby! If you don't release him right away, I won't listen to you anymore today." Mom pretended not hearing Isabelle's words and ate quietly. But she pricked her ears to listen to Ethan's cry. Ethan's cry is rhythmic and full of strength. There should be no worry for loss of breath.

Mom is curious in her mind: In ordinary days this little guy likes digging in Sister's room the best. He can find things to play with in every corner. Now being locked inside, why does he cry so earnestly? It's not even a dark room...He should have understood it's a punishment.

The little guy cried in the room for two minutes. There is no sign that he is going to stop or moderate it. Mom started to worry.

Isabelle was already outraged: "Release him, right now! At once! If you don't release him now, I will go and release him myself!" Mom took a glance at her and stood up to open the door for the poor little guy.

Once the door is open, Ethan stopped his cry instantly. He rushed into Mom's arms, held Mom's neck tight with both arms, stuck his face to Mom's face and called "Mama" for several times.

Mom said: "If you throw fork and spoon to the floor again, Mom will lock you in your sister's room like this again. No throwing to the floor again from now on, okay?" Ethan said: "Okay."

Mom put him back into his seat. Ethan sat and ate quietly. After eating with good behavior for a long while, the sister and brother meet each other's eyes, both of them gave out big grins. The little guy was itching to play the game again. He threw the spoon over on the table, looked at Isabelle and said: "Uh-oh—"

Isabelle smiled, sat up to pick the spoon from the table and put it back on his placemat. Ethan said happily: "Thanks!"

Mom pretended not seeing what had happened: These two little guys are a good couple. Just don't throw it to the floor.

世界有时残酷　但爱从未缺席

查尔斯

[美国]雪莉·杰克逊

这是我儿子劳里上幼儿园的第一天。他正式告别了灯芯绒背带裤扎围嘴的行头，换上了蓝色牛仔裤系腰带的装束。开学第一天的早上，我看着他和隔壁的小姐姐一起出门。在我看来，这一幕分明是在宣告我生命中一个时代的结束。我那嗓音甜美的托儿所小家伙将被一个穿着长长的裤子、走起路来大摇大摆的小屁孩所取代。而就在刚刚，这个小屁孩甚至忘记了在路的拐角处停下来跟我挥手告别。

他回到家时跟以前没什么两样，只听前门砰的一声打开了，他把帽子扔在地板上，声音突然变得刺耳，喊道："家里有人吗？"午餐时，他对爸爸出言不逊，还弄洒了小妹妹的奶瓶。"今天在幼儿园过得怎么样？"我问道，故意装出很随意的语气。"挺好的。"他说。"你学了什么？"爸爸问道。劳里冷冷地注视着爸爸，回答说："我没有学到没有的东西。""任何东西"我纠正道，"没有学到任何东西。"

"不过老师打了一个男孩的屁股。"劳里说，说话时嘴里还吃着面包和黄油。"因为他没规矩。"他补充说，嘴巴里塞得满满的。"他干了什么？"我问，"他是谁？"劳里想了想说："他叫查尔斯，没规矩。老师打了他的屁股，然后让他在角落里罚站。他也太没规矩了。""他干了什么?"我再次问道。但此时劳里已经从椅子上滑下来,拿起一块饼干,逃之夭夭了,根本不理会他爸爸还没说完的话:"小子,回来!"

第二天午餐时,劳里一坐下就开始说:"嗯,今天查尔斯又做坏事了。"他边说边笑,嘴咧得老大,"今天查尔斯把老师给打了。""天哪,"我说,"我猜他又被打屁股了吧?""肯定啊。"劳里说。"查尔斯为什么打老师?"我问道。"因为老师想让他用红色蜡笔涂色,"劳里说,"而查尔斯却想用绿色蜡笔涂色,所以他打了老师,然后他就被老师打屁股了。老师还对全班说谁也不许跟他玩,可是大家还是跟查尔斯照玩不误。"

第三天,也就是劳里上幼儿园第一周的星期三,我们听劳里说查尔斯又蹦又跳,把一个女孩的头撞流血了。老师罚他下课后不许离开教室。星期四,查尔斯在讲故事时间被老师罚站,因为他不停地跺地板。星期五,查尔斯被罚,被没收了黑板,因为他乱扔粉笔头。

"你觉得幼儿园会怎么处理查尔斯?"劳里爸爸问劳里。劳里故作深沉地耸了耸肩,说:"我猜他会被开除。"我们听劳里说,第二周的星期三和星期四跟平常一样:查尔斯在讲故事时间大喊大叫;打了一个男孩的肚子,还把他打哭了。星期五,查尔斯又一次被罚放学后不许回家,连累了全班同学。

从第三周开始,"查尔斯"已经成为我们家的"名人":整个下午,小妹妹都在哭闹,跟查尔斯一样;劳里把他的玩具货车装满泥巴在厨房里拖来拖去,跟查尔斯一样;甚至连孩子爸爸的肘部挂住电话线,然后把桌子上的电话、烟灰缸和一盆花都一股脑儿地带到了地板上,就在那一瞬间,他"看上去跟查尔斯一样"。

在第三周和第四周,我们听劳里说查尔斯似乎有了点悔改的意思。第三周的一天,在吃午饭的时候,劳里一脸严肃地汇报了查尔斯的近况:"查尔斯今天表现非常好,老师还奖励了他一个苹果。""什么?"我将信将疑地问。然后,我丈夫警惕地补充说:"你是说查尔斯吗?""就是查尔斯。"劳里回答说。"他帮老师分发了蜡笔,还帮老师收了作业。老师夸他是她的小助手。""发生了什么?"我将信将疑地问道。"他成了老师的小助手,就是这样。"劳里回答说,然后耸了耸肩。

"对于查尔斯来说,这可能是真的吗?"那天晚上我问丈夫,"这样的事情可能发生吗?""那就等着瞧呗。"我丈夫冷嘲热讽地说道。"当你要对付的是一个像查尔斯这样的孩子时,这可能意味着他只是在策划更多的捣蛋行动。"他说的似乎没错。因为一个星期还不到,一切又都恢复正常了,查尔斯依旧是原来那个可怕的捣蛋鬼。

"下周要开家长会了,"一天晚上,我告诉丈夫说,"我要在家长会上见见查尔斯的母亲。""问问她查尔斯身上究竟发生了什么。"我丈夫说。"我想知道怎么回事。"我说:"嗯,我也想知道。"

开家长会的那天晚上,我要出发时孩子爸爸送我到门口。"家长会结束后邀她出来喝杯茶,"他说,"我想见见她。""嗯,只要她到场。"我虔诚地说。"她肯定会去的,"我丈夫说,"我想象不到,如果查尔斯母亲不到场,他们怎么开这个家长会。"家长会上,我焦躁不安地坐在那里,用目光扫视着一张张轻松自在的脸庞,试图找辨认出哪张面庞的背后隐藏着查尔斯的秘密。

我们没有从任何一张脸上发现憔悴不堪,也没有人在会上站起来为她儿子的行为道歉,甚至没有人提到查尔斯。家长会结束后,我认出并找到了劳里的幼儿园老师。她手里拿着一个盘子,盘子上放着一杯茶和一块巧克力蛋糕;我手里的盘子里有一杯茶 块棉花糖蛋糕。

我们小心翼翼地朝着彼此走去,脸上带着笑。"我一直都很想见到您,"我说,"我是劳里的母亲。""我们都对劳里很感兴趣。"她说。

"嗯，他确实很喜欢幼儿园，"我说，"他一直都在跟我们说幼儿园的事情。""孩子刚上幼儿园一个星期左右，我们调整起来有点困难，"她拘谨地说，"但现在他已经成了一个很好的小助手。当然，偶尔也会出些小差池。""劳里通常会很快调整过来的，"我说，"我想有时候他可能是受了查尔斯的影响。""查尔斯？""是的，"我说着，不禁哈哈大笑起来，"您肯定在幼儿园被查尔斯这孩子搞得手忙脚乱吧。""查尔斯？"她说，"我们幼儿园没有叫查尔斯的啊。"

Charles

By Shirley Jackson

The day my son Laurie started kindergarten he renounced corduroy overalls with bibs and began wearing blue jeans with a belt; I watched him go off the first morning with the older girl next door, seeing clearly that an era of my life was ended, my sweet-voiced nursery-school tot replaced by a long-trousered, swaggering character who forgot to stop at the corner and wave good-bye to me.

He came home the same way, the front door slamming open, his cap on the floor, and the voice suddenly become raucous shouting: "Isn't anybody here?" At lunch he spoke insolently to his father and spilled his baby sister's milk. "How was school today?" I asked, elaborately casual. "All right," he said. "Did you learn anything?" his father asked. Laurie regarded his father coldly. "I didn't learn nothing," he said. "Anything," I said. "Didn't learn anything."

"The teacher spanked a boy, though," Laurie said, addressing his bread and butter. "For being fresh," he added, with his mouth full. "What did he do?" I asked. "Who was it?" Laurie thought. "It was Charles," he said. "He was fresh. The teacher spanked him and made him stand in a corner. He was awfully fresh." "What did he do?" I asked again, but Laurie slid off his chair, took a cookie, and left, while his father was still saying, "See here, young man."

The next day Laurie remarked at lunch, as soon as he sat down, "Well, Charles was bad again today." He grinned enormously and said, "Today Charles hit the teacher." "Good heavens," I said. "I suppose he got spanked again?" "He sure did," Laurie said. "Why did Charles hit the teacher?" I asked. "Because she tried to make him colour with red crayons," Laurie said. "Charles wanted to colour with green crayons so he hit the teacher and she spanked him and said nobody play with Charles but everybody did."

The third day—it was Wednesday of the first week—Charles bounced a see-saw on to the head of a little girl and made her bleed, and the teacher made him stay inside all during recess. Thursday Charles had to stand in a corner during story time because he kept pounding his feet on the floor. Friday Charles was deprived of blackboard privileges because he threw chalk.

"What are they going to do about Charles, do you suppose?" Laurie's father asked him. Laurie shrugged elaborately. "Throw him out of school, I guess," he said. Wednesday and Thursday were routine; Charles yelled during story hour and hit a boy in the stomach and made him cry. On Friday Charles stayed after school again and so did all the other children.

With the third week of kindergarten Charles was an institution in our family; the baby was being a Charles when she cried all afternoon; Laurie did a Charles when he filled his wagon full of mud and pulled it through the kitchen; even my husband, when he caught his elbow in the telephone cord and pulled telephone, ashtray, and a bowl of flowers off the table, said, after the first minute, "looks like Charles".

During the third and fourth weeks it looked like a reformation in Charles; Laurie reported grimly at lunch on Charles in the third week, "Charles was so good today the teacher gave him an apple." "What?" I said, and my husband added warily, "You mean Charles?" "Charles," Laurie said. "He gave the crayons around and he picked up the books afterward and the teacher said he was her helper." "What happened?" I asked incredulously. "He was her helper, that's all," Laurie said, and shrugged.

"Can this be true, about Charles?" I asked my husband that night. "Can something like this happen?" "Wait and see," my husband said cynically. "When you've got a Charles to deal with, this may mean he's only plotting." He seemed to be right. Within a week, everything was back to normal and Charles was his usual, terrible self.

"The Parent meeting's next week," I told my husband one

evening. "I'm going to find Charles's mother there." "Ask her what happened to Charles," my husband said. "I'd like to know." "I'd like to know myself," I said.

My husband came to the door with me that evening as I set out for the parent meeting. "Invite her over for a cup of tea after the meeting," he said. "I want to get a look at her." "If only she's there," I said prayerfully. "She'll be there," my husband said. "I don't see how they could hold a Parent meeting without Charles's mother." At the meeting I sat restlessly, scanning each comfortable matronly face, trying to determine which one hid the secret of Charles.

None of them looked to me haggard enough. No one stood up in the meeting and apologized for the way her son had been acting. No one mentioned Charles. After the meeting I identified and sought out Laurie's kindergarten teacher. She had a plate with a cup of tea and a piece of chocolate cake; I had a plate with a cup of tea and a piece of marshmallow cake.

We manoeuvred up to one another cautiously, and smiled. "I've been so anxious to meet you," I said. "I'm Laurie's mother." "We're all so interested in Laurie," she said. "Well, he certainly likes kindergarten," I said. "He talks about it all the time." "We had a little trouble adjusting, the first week or so," she said primly, "but now he's a fine little helper. With occasional lapses, of course." "Laurie usually adjusts very quickly," I said. "I suppose sometimes it's Charles's influence." "Charles?" "Yes," I said, laughing, "you must have your hands full in that kindergarten, with Charles." "Charles?" she said. "We don't have any Charles in the kindergarten."

离开比尔

[英国] 盖纳·黑尔

特鲁达犹豫着,还有多久她就该离开了?一个小时?两个小时?三个小时?三个小时。是的,为了安全起见。她上了台阶拉开了前门,就随手带上了门。

花园小道上黑白相间的方格瓷砖闪闪发光,天在下雨,脚下路滑。当特鲁达走到大门前时,停下了脚步,回头看着她身后那幢小小的联排房屋。三十年前他们搬到那里时她曾经有过种种憧憬。深绿色的大门上有两个黄铜的门环,房子因而看起来更加坚固可靠,是一个可以安居成家的可靠之地。然而三次流产后,她放弃了所有希望。

当然,那是比尔的错。特鲁达当时嫁给他,是因为不了解他。她的父亲是一个可爱的人,身材高挑颀长,一头银发,还有着一个温柔的灵魂。特鲁达的名字就是根据他的喜好起的。她的母亲曾经在一部战争片中见过一个叫特鲁达的角色,她深深地被这位女英雄的死亡悲剧所打动。当特鲁达出生时,她的父亲为了让妻子高兴而抛弃了自己的凯尔特人的传统和传统的家族姓氏。田园诗般的童年使得特鲁达对现实中的男人没有任何防备。

天空下着毛毛细雨,空气中升起一层薄雾,特鲁达调整了一下自己的头巾，不想让这种潮气破坏今早自己花了几个小时弄的卷发。她在昏暗中让自己振作精神，向大街走去。

二十分钟以后，特鲁达看到了奥黑尔家亮起来的灯，散发着金黄色的柔和的光，从一排四四方方的小窗户中透出来。报刊经销店看起来是那样温暖，充满魅力，就像迪肯小说里圣诞节的场景。特鲁达推开门，门口叮当响的欢快铃铛似乎在宣布着她的到来。

商店看起来空荡荡的，于是，特鲁达等待着，为打发时间，就仔细地看着柜台后面架子上陈列的一大罐闪闪发光的糖果。草莓的小糖果、大拇指汤姆的小果核、冬季混合剂、粉色的小虾米、飞碟、耐嚼的坚果……奥黑尔夫人缓慢地拖着脚步从陈列柜后边出来。"下午好啊，特鲁达。一切如常吗？"她问道。

特鲁达通常会从这里给比尔买烟，但是这一次要的是《广播时代》和四分之一磅柠檬果冻。奥黑尔夫人用她缓慢而颤抖的方式配好货。特鲁达伸出手付钱的时候，这个老妇人突然用力地抓着她的手说道："亲爱的，要照顾好自己。"接着，特鲁达感觉到门开了，身后突然一阵寒气袭来，伴随着铃铛声，另一位顾客进来了。她很感激这位顾客打断了这次对话，然后朝奥黑尔夫人温和地笑了笑，松开了她的手，转身溜回沉闷的街道上。

如果换作其他任何一天，特鲁达在离开商店时都会因羞愧而流泪。但是今天她没有这样，今天她在照顾自己了。她开始觉得自己的心情变得轻松了，就好像她踏上了另一个星球，在那里空气更稀薄，重力不会对她造成太大的压力。她看了看表。二十五分钟过去了。她取出一块柠檬果冻塞进嘴里，继续往前走。

特鲁达的嘴里充满了柠檬强烈的酸甜味道，此时，洒满阳光的花园，发出咕噜噜的叫声的矮脚鸡和父亲在发薪日带回来的零食，在特鲁达记忆里浮现。她有多久没吃甜食了？比尔不让她买任何奢侈品。他会说，如果她有钱买奢侈品，那么显然是她的钱太多了，而结果是，她那微薄的家用开支下个星期就会变少。不过，他买烟和苹果酒的钱却从来不缺。

尽管天空中的毛毛雨越下越大，特鲁达还是稍微放慢了脚步，但她仍然还有两个半小时要打发，在比尔走了之前她当然不想回家。

十分钟后，特鲁达发现自己走到了奥斯特莱特咖啡馆外面。荧光灯从咖啡馆里照射到泥泞的人行道上，但是咖啡馆的窗户却是阴沉沉的、模糊不清的，让特鲁达无法看清里面。于是，她用力推开门，马上就感受到了屋里闷热潮湿的热情欢迎氛围。

咖啡馆里的座位大约坐满了一半，由于谈话声和餐具发出的叮当响，咖啡馆里熙熙攘攘。没有人注意到特鲁达进来了。她，一个中年妇女，独自一人朝里边走去，她的身材并不显眼，因此不会引起别人的注意，不会造成任何干扰。当她小心翼翼地走近柜台时，新鲜的熏肉的烟熏香味在她周围的空气中弥漫开来。

柜台里的侍者比特鲁达高挑，比特鲁达年轻，很性感迷人，但是举止动作却硬邦邦的，与她柔软诱人的身材不配。特鲁达猜想她年轻时一定很漂亮，但是现在，她染过的头发看起来显得很阴暗，口红的颜色相对于她惨白的皮肤来说又太红了。她看着特鲁达迟迟疑疑地走过来，那张噘着的嘴和呆板的表情没有一丝一毫的变化，问道："需要点什么？"特鲁达点了一份冰面包和一杯热可可。"我这就给你去拿。"侍者说道。特鲁达很庆幸这个女人表现出日常的漫不经心的态度。

她找了一张两人用的福米加牌塑料贴面的小餐桌，在一把硬硬的橙色塑料椅子上缓缓坐下。她开始感到疼痛，搏动的太阳穴发出熟悉的节奏。她这次回家后要洗个长长的热水澡。而不是像平时在比尔把水用得差不多了以后,给她只剩下两英寸的温水。她要好好泡一个泡泡浴。

侍者唐突地将特鲁达点的东西送了上来,脸上还是面无表情。那个冰面包看起来稍微有些硬,可可很稀,但是她来这样一个便宜的咖啡馆就是为了偷得浮生半日闲,这是她延缓回家的唯一去处,而不是为了吃东西。她曾经有过一些朋友,但是比尔的粗鲁无礼和喜怒无常让朋友们和他们逐渐疏远了。

冰面包有点黏,于是,特鲁达四处张望看看能不能找到餐巾纸。她发现在远处的一张桌子上一群工人正在看着她。他们看起来有些眼熟,她想,或许他们是跟比尔在建筑工地一起工作的人,所以这就是他们为什么会在下午三点左右在这个咖啡馆里出现,是因为天气恶劣,工地白天停工。当他们意识到特鲁达已经注意到他们时,他们齐刷刷地迅速低下了头。他们默默地吃着眼前盘子里的东西,特鲁达想他们中间有人微微红了脸。她不知道自己是否需要补妆。

为了避免进一步的尴尬,特鲁达的目光一直盯着咖啡馆的窗户。其实她看不太清楚,窗户的玻璃上凝结了一层薄薄的水珠,模糊了她看向外面世界的视线。特鲁达试着去想象她现在的生活将会发生怎样的变化,但在除了接下来的几个小时的事情,似乎看起来都是模模糊糊的,一如她隐藏在云山雾罩的玻璃后面的未来。她现在只要一想到今天晚上的事就很满足。她今天一大早就放好了燃料,只需要一根火柴就能点燃卷起的报纸,炉火马上就会燃烧起来。这样今天晚上等她洗完澡,房子就暖和了。然后她坐下来看电视,她的脚放在凳子上,将编织物放在膝盖上。她要吃光柠檬果冻,除了她自己,不需要取悦任何人。想到这些,她心花怒放,她记起了什么是幸福。

咖啡馆的墙上挂着一个方形的、发着光的钟。特鲁达从她坐着的地方可以清楚地看到那些大大的、鲜艳的蓝色数字。半个小时过去了,她已经吃完了她点的餐,她尽所能往远处看去。还有足够的时间再喝一杯热可可,看看《广播时代》。

喝完第二杯热可可后,特鲁达勇敢地迎着陌生人凝视和同情的目光去买了点东西。埃德·特纳和他的儿子,瑞奇,在肉店里做服务生。

当她走近时,埃德给了她一个悲伤的微笑,平静地说道:"看来你需要一份好牛排。"

特鲁达回答道:"请给我两份排骨,埃德。"

她注意到,埃德在她的单子里额外加了几块排骨,她担心自己可能会哭出来,于是将自己的注意力转向了远处柜台的那一头。瑞奇正在为庄园里的一位年轻妈妈服务。在递给她一磅香肠时,他朝着那个咯咯笑的女人闪过一个灿烂的微笑,眨了眨眼。这就像比尔一样。

特鲁达和比尔是在特拉法加相遇的。她在工作中交了一个新朋友,名叫佩格,佩格说服了她在那个星期六晚上出去玩。特鲁达的母亲说佩格是"最棒的",特鲁达在她的陪伴下感到有点紧张。她跟在佩格身后走到吧台前,用指尖紧紧抓住她朋友那件薄薄的衬衫下摆。当她胆怯地走进陌生的环境时,比尔抓住了她的眼球,朝她眨了眨眼睛。后来他又抓住了她的心。

比尔的眼睛就像冬日里的淡蓝色的天空,与浓密黑色的睫毛形成了鲜明的对比,这让比尔的目光看起来更加热切,令人紧张不安。在夏日的阳光下,他用砖斗扛着红砖和水泥,深棕色的身体肌肉发达。特鲁达从未见过如此自信的人,如此确定他们的价值和应得的东西。当她和他在一起的时候,她感到不那么害怕,也不那么害怕这个世界。由于盲目的爱情,她把他的傲慢误认为是自信,把他的虚荣误认为是自重。

在他们结婚后的一周,特鲁达发现她长了疥疮。比尔告诉她,自己一定是在马桶座圈上被传染的,但是佩格马上就把这个说法拨乱反正了。她在那天看清了比尔，但是不论是好是坏，一切都太晚了。

接着咯咯笑变成了嘎嘎的笑声和呼唤，让特鲁达回到了现实里。她将排骨放进包里，谢过埃德后，继续逛着超市。总之，她打算在这里再打发掉二十分钟。

特鲁达选了一条更远的路回家，她放慢脚步试图来掩饰自己加快的脉搏跳动速率。即使是这样，在她到家的时候距离三个小时还是差了二十分钟。天渐渐黑了下来，在街灯的映照下，漂着油污的沟里出现了彩虹。所有的一切看起来都是那么安详。特鲁达看到并没有灯光从房子里照出来。特鲁达停在大门前，试图平复自己加速的心跳。

在她打开前门的时候，特鲁达神经紧张地听着有没有人的动静。寂静一片。前厅里的照明开关一闪一闪的，显示着所有的事物都和她离开时一样。他难道已经走了？特鲁达缩了缩身子，放下购物袋，挂起外套，每一个动作都在让她回想起早晨受到的攻击。她转身面向镜子摘下头巾，下意识地啜泣了一声，她连忙用手捂住了嘴。她的眼睛肿得像熟了的紫红色的李子那么大，而这片紫红色已经蔓延到了太阳穴和脸颊。她的眼睛因为肿胀几乎盖过了一切，她能看到一抹深红色的闪光染红了她的眼白。这还不是比尔发脾气以后她最糟糕的样子，但这是最近发生的事。

特鲁达朝着厨房走去。她看到比尔的脚从厨房的餐桌后伸了出来，他的工作短袜上还沾着工地上的沙子和水泥。他工作回家后从来不换袜子，而是拖着脚在家里到处走，把家里弄得满地是泥。直到吃完晚餐，要去洗澡了，他才会将袜子脱下来。她离得比尔更近一些，这样就能看见他的全身。他毫无疑问已经走了，千真万确。她以前见过死人。她的父亲是在一天晚上熟睡时死的，特鲁达次日去公寓里看他的时候发现的。他坐在单人扶手椅里，头向前耷拉着，好像在打盹，身边的桌子上放着一杯喝了一半的热可可。

比尔的结局并不好。他在上午九点钟回来的时候,因为失去了白天的工作而感到很愤怒,手提着两公升的苹果酒。特鲁达知道接下来会发生些什么,一个小时之后,事情就发生了。在挨过第一拳之后,她转头面向着厨房的墙壁,以便支撑着自己,准备好迎接猛攻,可是他接着又打了几拳。过了一会儿,特鲁达才意识到比尔停止了对自己的攻击,等她转过身后,她看到比尔跪在她的眼前。他的半边脸耷拉下来,像烈日下的一根蜡烛一样静静地融化了。

她清楚发生了什么。隔壁的杰克逊先生去年就中风了。后来虽然康复了,但是他的脸仍然看起来有点不对称。杰克逊夫人曾称赞救护车人员如此迅速地到达她的丈夫身边,中风后的每一分钟都很宝贵。你需要尽快得到救助。

特鲁达看到比尔斜向一边倒在地板上。他的眼睛苍白如水,眼睛睁着,眼神里有一丝恐惧一闪而过。她本想靠近他,帮助他,但当他们的目光相遇时,她看到恐惧过去了,怨恨回来了。

她转过身去取大衣。她该离开多久呢?

Leaving Bill

By Gaynor Hill

Truda hesitated, how much time should she leave? An hour? Two hours? Three hours? Three hours. Yes, just to be on the safe side. She stepped out onto the doorstep pulling the front door closed behind her.

The black and white chequered tiles of the garden path glistened, slick under her feet with the wet day. Truda paused when she got to the gate and looked back at her little terraced house. She'd had such hopes when they'd moved there thirty years ago. The dark green door with its brass knocker had made the house look solid and reliable, a safe place to set up home and start a family. Three miscarriages later, she'd given up hopes.

It was Bill's fault of course. Truda had married him because she hadn't known any better. Her father had been a lovely man, tall, thin, silver haired, a gentle soul. Truda had been named as a result of his indulgence. Her mother had seen a character called Truda in a war film and been touched by the tragedy of the heroine's demise. When Truda was born, her father had forsaken his Celtic heritage and the tradition of family names for the sake of his wife's happiness. An idyllic childhood had done nothing to prepare Truda for the reality of men.

Drizzle misted the air and Truda adjusted her headscarf not wanting the damp to undo the several hours in curlers she'd endured that morning. Bracing herself against the gloom, she set off in the direction of the high street.

Twenty minutes later Truda could see the lights of O'Hare's, glowing soft and golden through rows of small, square window panes. The Newsagents looked warm and inviting like something out of a Christmas scene in a Dicken's novel. Truda pushed the door open and, the merry jingle of the shop bell announced her arrival.

The shop appeared empty so Truda waited, occupying the time by perusing the large jars of sparkling sweets displayed on the shelves behind the counter. Strawberry bonbons, tom thumb pips, winter mixture, pink shrimps, flying saucers, chewy nuts…Mrs. O'Hare slowly shuffled into view from behind a display case. "Good afternoon, Truda. Your usual?" she asked.

Truda usually bought Bill's tobacco from O'Hare's but this time asked for the Radio Times and a quarter of sherbet lemons. Mrs. O'Hare made up and bagged the order in her slow and trembling way. As Truda reached out to pay, the old lady grasped her hand with sudden strength and said, "Do take care of yourself, dear." Behind her, Truda felt a rush of cold air as the shop door opened and another customer entered to the jingle of the bell. Grateful for the interruption she smiled softly at Mrs. O'Hare and, releasing her hand, turned and slipped back out onto the leaden street.

Any other day, Truda would have left the shop feeling ashamed and tearful. But not today, today she was taking care of herself. She had started to feel lighter as though she had stepped onto another planet where the air was thinner and gravity didn't press so heavily upon her. She checked her watch. Twenty-five minutes. She popped a sherbet lemon into her mouth and set off again.

Truda's mouth flooded with the sweet, sharp flavour of the sherbet lemon and it surfaced memories of a sunlit garden, purring bantams and her father bringing treats home on pay day. How long since she'd had sweets? Bill wouldn't let her buy anything in the way of luxuries. He'd say, if she had money for luxuries she obviously had too much, and her meagre housekeeping money would be lighter the next week as a result. There was always enough money for his tobacco and cider though.

Despite the thickening drizzle, Truda slowed her pace a little. She still had two and a half hours to kill and she certainly didn't want to get back home until Bill was gone.

Ten minutes later, Truda found herself outside the Astalet

Café. The fluorescent light from inside spilled out onto the puddled pavement but the windows were cloudy and opaque, preventing her from seeing inside. She had to push hard against the door to open it but was immediately rewarded for the effort by the steamy, welcoming warmth within.

The Café was about half full, noisy with conversation and the clinking of cutlery. No one looked up as Truda entered. With her head down, her lone, middle-aged, female form was too unremarkable to cause interruption. The smoky aroma of crisping bacon curled through the air around her as she cautiously approached the counter.

The waitress behind the counter was taller and younger than Truda, voluptuous but with a hardness of demeanour that didn't match her soft, inviting form. Truda thought she must have been beautiful in her youth, but now her dyed hair was a shade too dark and her lipstick a shade too red for the pallor of her skin. She looked up at Truda's hesitant approach and, without even the slightest change to her fixed and pursed expression asked, "Yes please?" Truda ordered an iced bun and a cup of hot chocolate. "I'll bring it over," said the waitress. Truda was thankful for the woman's casual indifference.

She found a small Formica table for two and eased herself down into one of the hard, orange, plastic chairs. She had started to ache and the throbbing at her temple drummed a familiar rhythm.

She would have a long, hot bath when she got home. Not the two inches of tepid water she was usually left with after Bill had exhausted the immersion. A nice, deep bath with bubbles.

The waitress delivered Truda's order abruptly and with the same impassive expression. The bun looked a little hard and the chocolate thin but these stolen half hours in cheap cafés had become her only respite from home and it was that, rather than the food, that she came for. She'd had friends once but Bill, boorish and volatile, had driven them all away.

The bun was sticky so Truda looked around to see whether there were any serviettes. She noticed a group of workmen at a far table looking at her. They seemed vaguely familiar and she thought that perhaps they worked with Bill on the construction site. That would explain why they were in the Café mid-afternoon, work on the site having been halted that morning due to the bad weather. The workmen looked down quickly and in unison as soon as they realised she'd noticed them. They silently busied themselves with the plates before them and Truda fancied that one of them reddened a little. She wondered whether she needed to touch up her makeup.

To avoid any further embarrassment, Truda fixed her gaze on the Café window. She couldn't see much, condensation filmed the panes blurring her view of the world outside. Truda tried to think about how her life would change now but anything beyond the next few hours seemed hazy and unclear as though her future also lay beyond the cloudy glass. She contented herself with thinking about the evening. She had laid a fire early this morning. It only needed a match to its rolled up newspaper bed and it would be roaring in no time. She'd light the fire first so that the house would be warm by the time she'd had her bath. Then she'd settle to watch the television, her feet up on the stool and her knitting in her lap. She'd have her sherbet lemons to finish and no one to please but herself. Her heart rose and she remembered what it was to be happy.

A square, illuminated clock hung on the Café wall. Truda could see the large bright blue numbers clearly from where she sat. Half an hour had passed whilst she'd finished her food and looked as far ahead as she was able. Plenty of time for another hot chocolate and a look through the Radio Times.

After her second hot chocolate Truda braved the stares and sympathies of strangers to do her little bit of shopping. Ed Turner and his son, Ricky, were serving in the butchers.

Ed gave her a sad smile as she approached. "Looks like you need a good steak," he said quietly.

"Just two chops please, Ed," Truda replied.

She noticed Ed adding a couple of extra chops to her order and worried that she might cry, turned her attention to the far end of the counter. Ricky was serving one of the young mums from the Estate. He flashed a sparkling smile at the giggling woman and winked as he handed over a pound of sausages. Just like Bill.

Truda had met Bill in the Trafalgar. She had made a new friend at work, Peg, who had persuaded her to go out that Saturday night. Truda's mother said Peg was "no better than she should be" and Truda had felt a little nervous in her company. She had walked up to the bar behind Peg, holding on tightly to the hem of her friend's flimsy blouse with her fingertips. As she timidly took in the unfamiliar surroundings, Bill had caught her eye and winked. Later he had caught her heart.

Bill's eyes were the pale blue of a winter sky and their contrast against his thick dark lashes made his gaze intense and unnerving. His body was muscle hard and nut brown from carrying hods of red brick and cement in the summer sun. Truda had never met anyone so self-assured, so certain of their worth and their due. When she was with him she felt less fearful, less daunted by the world. Love-blind she mistook his arrogance for confidence and his vanity for self-belief.

A week after their wedding Truda found she had scabies. Bill told her she must have caught them from a toilet seat but Peg soon put her right about that. She saw him clearly that day but it was too late, for better for worse.

The giggle became a cackle summoning Truda back to the present. She put the chops in her bag, thanked Ed and continued with her tour of the shops. All in all, she managed to kill another twenty minutes.

Truda took the longer route home, her slowing steps belying her increasing pulse rate. Even so, she was twenty minutes short of the three hours by the time she reached the house. It was getting dark and the street lights had come on revealing rainbows in the oil flecked gutters below. Everything seemed quiet and Truda couldn't see any light coming from inside the house. She paused at the gate and tried to calm her racing heart.

As she opened the front door, Truda strained to hear any suggestion of life within. Silence. A flick of the hall light switch revealed things to be exactly as she'd left them. Had he gone? Truda winced as she put down her shopping bag and hung up her coat, every movement now recalling the morning's assault. She turned towards the mirror to take off her headscarf and clasped her hand to her mouth to mute an involuntary sob. Her eyelid had swollen to the size and hue of a ripe plum and the colour had bled across her temple and cheek. Almost hidden by the swelling, she could see a flash of crimson staining the white of her eye. It wasn't the worst she'd looked after Bill had lost his temper but it came pretty close.

Truda walked towards the kitchen. She could see Bill's feet sticking out from behind the kitchen table, his work socks still crusted with sand and concrete from the site. He never changed his socks when he got home from work but traipsed muck through the whole house until after supper when he went up for a bath. She moved closer so that she could see the whole of him. He'd gone alright, well and truly. She'd seen death before. Her father had died in his sleep one evening and Truda had found him the next day when she went to the flat to check on him. He was sitting in his armchair with his head bent forward as though dozing, a half finished cup of cocoa on the table beside him.

Bill had not made a good end. He'd come home mid-morning, angry about losing the day's work and toting a two litre bottle of cider. Truda had known what was coming and an hour later it did. After the first blow she'd turned to the kitchen wall and braced herself for the onslaught but he'd only landed a few more punches. It had taken a moment for Truda to realise he'd stopped and, when she'd turned around, she'd seen him sinking to his knees before her. One side of his face was drooping like a candle softly melting in the hot sun.

She'd known what was happening. Mr. Jackson next door had suffered a stroke last year. He had recovered but his face still looked a little uneven. Mrs. Jackson had lauded the ambulance men for reaching her husband so quickly, every minute counted with a stroke. You had to get help quickly.

Truda had watched Bill fall sideways to the floor. His eyes, pale as water, had been open and there had been a flash of fear in them.

She'd made to move toward him, to help him, but as their eyes met she'd seen the fear pass and malevolence return.

She'd turned away to fetch her coat. How much time should she leave?

老照片

[印度] 希拉·马诺哈尔

"哦,天哪——房间里又乱成了一团!不,妈妈,不要再翻啦!请你搞清楚,你要找的那张照片根本就不在这个房子里。妈妈,拜托你不要把屋里翻得乱七八糟的,你这样做是给我添乱找事,我收拾不过来,累死人了啦!"珍妮一边说,一边寻思着从哪儿入手收拾。架子上文件夹里的纸撒得到处都是,大衣橱里的衣服扔得满房间都是。10岁儿子赖安的玩具箱翻了个底朝天,里面的玩具统统都倒在地上,书桌也被推开了。

珍妮的妈妈玛丽亚夫人今年已经78岁了,她的皮肤皱皱巴巴的,双目无神,但眼神里有一丝光闪烁着坚定的信念:她最终会找到那张老照片的!那是她和丈夫斯蒂夫的第一张夫妻合影。照片的背景就是那座漂亮的教堂,他们就在那座教堂里举行的婚礼。

他们结婚已经52年了。

事实上,有很长一段时间玛丽亚也把这张照片忘得干干净净。两年前,病入膏肓的丈夫拉着她的手,说他这辈子能娶她为妻是多么幸运,回忆起结婚的日子。他告诉她在离开这个世界之前,他最想看到的就是那张和她合影的照片。就这样,玛丽亚寻找老照片的行动开始了。

斯蒂夫去世以后，玛丽亚搬到女儿珍妮家住。尽管她脑海里对那张照片到底在哪儿一点印象都没有，但是她还是不停地找，不放过任何一个角落。结果呢，就是把房间弄得乱七八糟，珍妮的丈夫对玛丽亚发飙。看到丈夫对母亲大喊大叫，珍妮感到心烦意乱，也无可奈何。她对妈妈解释过成千上万遍：那张老照片早已经被他们弄丢了，怎么找也找不到的。可是妈妈始终不放弃，她总是说最终会找到那张照片的。

"赖安，好好地待在家里，照顾好姥姥，不要打扰她。我们很快就会回来。爱你。"珍妮向儿子交代了几句，然后和丈夫坐进了汽车，他们要去参加一场宴会。他们的车子刚一离开，10岁的赖安便回了屋，拉着姥姥的手问她一直在找什么。玛丽亚给外孙讲了那张老照片的故事。赖安把她拉到沙发上坐下，然后对她说："姥姥，你不要着急，我来帮你找。告诉我，你到这里和我妈妈住在一起的时候，都带着哪些东西过来的？"玛丽亚认真地回忆了一会儿，告诉外孙她来的时候带的东西很少，只有换洗衣服、首饰和药这些生活必需品。她说老房子里其余的东西都是珍妮处理的，她说她见过珍妮从老房子里拿出来一个棕色包，却不知道里面装的是什么，也不知道这个包现在放在哪里。

听罢，赖安立刻出了屋，搬进来一个梯子，然后他顺着梯子爬上了阁楼。他开始在阁楼上寻找那个棕色包。他在那里发现了许多包和盒子，就一个个地挪到一边。终于在墙角找到了满是灰尘的棕色包。赖安把棕色包拎出来，打开。他在包里发现了许多文件、报纸、杂志、信件，就是没有那张老照片。他还在棕色包里找到一把钥匙，可是却不知道它能够打开哪把锁。赖安垂头丧气地走出阁楼，抬腿的时候，不小心被一个手提箱绊了一下，差点儿摔倒。赖安好奇地拎起手提箱一看，发现箱子上着锁。他用那把找到的钥匙试了一下，谁知竟然把锁打开了，让他大吃一惊。他开始仔细地检查手提箱里的每一件东西。他发现了一本书，书皮上有标签，标签上写着：一年级学生珍妮·科林斯的图画本。赖安打开图画本，看到了妈妈小时候画的各种各样的图画。赖安飞快地翻阅着这本图画本，在它的最后一页他看到了一张照片。赖安拿起这张照片仔细地端详：照片上有一个漂亮的女孩，一只手拿着一束花，另一只手被一个英俊的小伙子挽着。背景是一座漂亮的教堂，有人在照片的后面写了这样一句话："玛丽亚、斯蒂夫结婚纪念照——摄于1960年8月8日。"赖安知道这就是玛丽亚一直苦苦寻找的那张照片！他飞快地从阁楼上跑下来，边跑边喊："姥姥，我找到了……我找到了！"这个时候，珍妮刚进家门，正好听到儿子大声的叫喊。她问赖安发生了什么。赖安讲述了他翻阁楼找到了玛丽亚遍寻不见的老照片。他们俩兴奋地进屋给玛丽亚看。

可是，他们惊骇万分地看到玛丽亚躺在地板上，昏迷不醒。他们赶紧把她送到了医院。通过检查，医生说她的心脏病突然发作，病情严重。赖安请求医生让他见姥姥一面。赖安坐在姥姥的床边，凑在姥姥的耳朵旁边轻轻地说道："姥姥，你看这张照片上的你好漂亮啊！还有姥爷……那句话怎么说来着？哦，对了——他是我见过的最帅的小伙子！姥姥，你同意吧？姥姥，你睁开眼睛再看看姥爷……姥爷正在对你笑呢！"

忍着全身巨大的疼痛，玛丽亚用尽全身的力气睁开了双眼，眼睛闪闪发亮，她又看了一眼这张老照片，然后永远地合上了双眼。

The Photograph

By Sheela Manohar

"Oh GOD…the room is a mess again. No mom. Not again. Please try to understand that the photo you are searching is not there in this house. So please mom don't make a mess of everything and give me more work. I can't clean this up. It's tiring." Jenny spoke as she wondered where she should start the cleaning up. The papers from the files in the rack lay in all directions. The clothes from the closet were thrown everywhere in the room. 10-year-old Ryan's toy basket was lying upside down with the toys strewn around. The study table was pushed away.

Jenny's mom Maria was a 78-year-old lady. Her skin was wrinkled out and her eyes pale. But there was a glow and determination in her eyes that she would find the photograph one day. The first photo which she and Steve had got clicked as a husband and wife in the backdrop of the beautiful church where their wedding took place.

It was 52 years since their marriage.

In fact Maria had herself long forgotten about the photo. It was only 2 years back when Steve was in a critical condition in the hospital that he held Maria's hand and said how lucky he was to have her as his wife and remembered their wedding days. He had told he would love to see that photograph before passing away. Maria's search for the photo began then.

Even though Maria lived in daughter Jenny's house after Steve passed away and she didn't even have a faint idea as to where the photo would be, she would search every nook and corner of Jenny's house for the photo. It resulted in the house being a mess and often Jenny's husband would get mad at Maria. Jenny would be disturbed to see her mom being shouted at and yet would feel helpless. She had tried a thousand ways to explain to her mom that they had lost the photo long ago and they would not find it no matter what. But Maria was not the one to give up. She would say that she will find the photo one day.

"Ryan, take care of yourself and grandma. Don't trouble her. We will be back soon. Love you." Jenny said as she got in to the car with her husband to attend a party. As soon as they were off, Ryan came inside the home, held Maria's hands and asked her what is it that she keeps searching all the time. Maria told him about the photo. Ryan made her sit on the sofa and said, "Don't worry grandma. I will help you find it. Tell me what are the things you got when you moved in here with mom?" Maria tried hard to remember and told him she had very few stuff like her clothes, her jewellery, her medicines and few other necessary things. She said she did not know what Jenny did with the rest. She said she had seen Jenny carrying a brown colour bag from her house, but didn't know what was in it or where it was.

Ryan immediately walked out and got the ladder and climbed up the attic. He started searching for the brown bag. He discovered too many bags and boxes there and started moving each one aside. The brown bag lay in a corner amidst lots of dust. He picked it up and opened it. He found files, papers, magazines, letters everything but not the photo. He also found a key in the bag, but could not find out to which lock it belonged. Disappointed he started walking out of the attic. As he stepped out, his legs stumbled on a suitcase. Curious, he took it to see it locked. He tried opening it with the key he found there and to his surprise it opened. He started searching everything in the suitcase. He found a book. The label on the book said Jennifer Collins, Class 1, drawing book. He opened it to see various drawings his mom had done as a child. As he flipped to the last page, he saw a photo. He took the photo in his hand. The photo had a beautiful young girl holding flowers in one hand and the other hand held by a handsome man. There was a beautiful church in the backdrop. Somebody had written on the back of the photo "Maria weds Steve—8th August 1960". Ryan knew it was this photo that Maria was searching all along and ran down shouting: "Grandma, I got it...I got it." Jenny entered the house to the screams of Ryan and asked him what happened. Ryan told he searched the attic and found the photo Maria was looking for. Excited, both of them rushed to the room to show it to Maria.

They were shocked to see Maria lying on the floor. They rushed her to the hospital. The doctors said she had suffered a heart attack and was serious. Ryan pleaded with the doctors to let him see his grandma once. He sat by his grandma on the bed and whispered in her ears: "Grandma, you look so beautiful in this picture and about grandpa...well what to say about him...he is the most handsome man I've ever seen. Don't you agree? Just see him once...he is smiling at you."

With all the pain her body was going through, Maria opened her sparkling eyes. She saw the photo once before closing her eyes forever.

黑色面纱

[美国]卡桑德拉·琼斯

海文·桑顿－米尔斯站在高档红木度假村外昏暗的阴影里,当看到与她结婚二十七年的丈夫挽着他的新情妇从奢华的铜门里走出来时,她精致的五官罩上了一副冰冷的面具。他孩子气地咧嘴一笑,昂首阔步,海文的脑海里确定无疑地脑补出刚刚关上的门后发生过的内容。布雷特拥着这个看上去比他年轻一半的女人,这时,司机把他的车开过来,这辆该死的车花了海文一大笔钱。然而,那个女人神态自若地上了车,就好像这辆车和这个男人归她所有似的。布雷特卑鄙无耻、花天酒地的生活方式不仅仅浪费了海文的钱,还玷污了她的名声,让她的骄傲像受伤的动物一样流血,仅存的这点自尊也微不足道了。但今晚,这一切就要停止了。

海文把淡紫色的毛衣披在纤细的肩上以抵御傍晚的寒意。她回到候在一边的豪华轿车里。当她坐在柔软的皮革座椅上,交叉着长腿,手里拿着香槟时,司机拉开了中间的窗户。他金色的眼睛赞赏地凝视着她的黑色长裙和透明丝袜。有那么一瞬间,海文忘记了布雷特和他的姘头,让自己沉浸在一个男人对她日渐衰老的美貌的欣赏之中。尽管这位皮肤黝黑、肌肉发达的司机太年轻了,而且她永远不会与员工跨过那道线，但他仍然刺激了她的性欲，虽然在法律上她宣称她的性欲已经死亡。

"跟着他？"他问。

海文的嘴唇绷得紧紧的。她只是点了点头，把凝视的目光投向了酒店的原始财产，那里倾斜的、郁郁葱葱的景观和新奇物品商店很快就从视野中消失了，豪华轿车保持着安全距离，追赶着布雷特。

在布雷特搞出无数桃色事件之前，海文心中的黑洞曾经充满了无穷无尽的爱。在她腰缠万贯的父亲温德尔·桑顿的庇护下，加上她缺少与男人打交道的经验，她一看到布雷特那双炯炯有神的绿眼睛，就被他狡诈的魅力吸引了。与他相识还不到六个月，他们就不顾她父亲的反对，结了婚。

在威斯康星州新里斯本这样的小镇上，谣言像野火一样蔓延开来，没过多久她就发现了他对女人和精致生活的贪得无厌。以牺牲海文为代价，布雷特继续招蜂引蝶，从世界上最好的大学获得了三个学位，现在已经56岁的他，仍然不知道他的人生想做什么。最让她痛苦的是他拒绝生孩子，而现在她的生物钟早已走到尽头，永远不可能生儿育女了。尽管如此，她自始至终都爱着他。

然而，今晚，当她望着前方夜空下爱人的剪影轮廓时，对丈夫却只有厌恶、蔑视。她想象着布雷特夹在女人的两腿之间，口吐白沫，像一条发情的狗一样骑在她身上，忘记了他神圣的婚姻誓言和给他一切的妻子。一股新的怒火从她的灵魂深处升起，愤怒使她盲目，复仇使她不顾一切。她把香槟酒玻璃杯扔进侧窗，把它摔得粉碎。他怎么敢这样？他以为他是谁？

"一切都顺利吗？"对讲机里传来了那个平静的声音。

海文的五脏六腑在翻江倒海，她感到不舒服。呼吸也不匀了，她从钱包里拿出化妆盒,往鼻子上扑了点粉。

"米尔斯夫人?"

"我很好,开你那该死的车吧。"

她伸出手,从碎冰里拿出一瓶香槟,倾斜到嘴边。满是泡沫的液体在她的嘴边咕噜咕噜地作响,酒劲上了头。她又拿了一瓶香槟酒,但当豪华轿车在一条黑暗、不祥的街道上停下来时,她的整个身体都僵直了。她慢慢地把瓶子放在一边,眼睛盯着布雷特的车。是用她的钱买的这栋房子吗?一扇铁门开了,他可以进入这栋令人印象深刻、保存完好的房子,它坐落在宛若糖枫树拼贴出的拼贴画里。布雷特把车停在环形车道上,从驾驶座上爬出来,去扶那个女人下车。他们为一个别人听不懂的或只能私下讲的笑话咯咯地笑着,热烈地接吻,然后他拉起她的手,消失在一个爬满玫瑰的拱形入口。

似乎过了很久,海文才瞥了一眼她镶满钻石的手表——其实才过了一个小时。她用戴着手套的手扯了扯金色的假发,确保她栗色的头发不会掉出来。

该动手了。

她推开豪华轿车的门,走了出来,朝房子走去。她的脚跟轻轻地踏在鹅卵石路上发出咔嗒咔嗒的声音。她拉了拉大门,惊喜地发现门没锁。她从那个小门缝溜了进去,急忙跑到布雷特的车旁等着。

十五分钟后,布雷特终于吹着口哨踏出家门。他离她越近,她的心就越沉重,因为她知道他们的生命将在今晚结束,而当她知道他曾尽其所能地利用过她时,她的心就更加沉重了。

布雷特吓了一跳,气喘吁吁地倒退着。"海文,你——你在这儿干什么?"

风中传来一股淡淡的女人香水的味道,考虑到那不是她的,海文做出唯一明智的假设。"我应该问你这个问题。你在这儿干什么？"

"我来送一个朋友。她被困住了……"

"布雷特，别侮辱我的智商，因为我们都知道她只是你这辈子谎言里的另一个破鞋。"

他朝车走去，他的眼睛闪着怒火。"我们回家讨论这件事。"

海文没了耐心。"你没有家。你有的只是身上皮，对此你也要心存感激。"她把手伸进钱包，掏出一张纸和一支笔。"签名。"她厉声说。

他咯咯地笑了。"你真的认为我有那么蠢吗？要摆脱我可没那么容易。我已经习惯了这种有利可图的生活方式，不管我们是否在一起，我都希望这种生活方式能继续下去。所以，回家吧，回到属于你的地方。我会去那里看你。"

"这是你最后的机会。签了字，我就给你10万美元，然后悄悄离婚。"

"你可真可怜。没有男人会再需要你了。"

她从来没有像现在这样恨他。"你是对的。嫁给你这样一个失败者，我是很可怜。至于另一个人，很多人都在翘首以待来取代你的位置，包括你最好的朋友。"她把纸放回钱包。"我的报价过期了。"

布雷特脸色苍白，嘴唇扭曲，邪恶地咆哮起来："你是个干瘪的老太婆，哈罗德不会要你的。"

"他已经要了。"她转身走下车道。虽然她谎称和哈罗德上床，但布雷特脸上的惊讶表情弥补了他轻易造成的痛苦。

布雷特在她身后喊道："这段婚姻已经走到了尽头。此外，我和卡罗尔想在一起。两百万美元，我会安静地离开。"她尽最大努力不去理会他，但听到他提到另一个女人的名字时，简直就是在扎她的心。

海文回到豪华轿车里，回头看了布雷特最后一眼，看到他在上车。

"开到下一个街区。"她命令司机。他们一就位,她就从钱包里拿出一个银色的扁平装置。她的手指停了下来,最后一次仔细思考她的决定。羞辱、痛苦和愤怒给了她所需的勇气。她按下了按钮。震耳欲聋的爆炸声打破了附近的平静,一团隆隆作响的火球划破天空,散成多个小火球,小火球后面拖着浓烟。豪华轿车下面的地面震动了;一盏街灯忽明忽暗,然后把他们投进一片漆黑之中。豪华轿车加快了速度向前进。

走了一小段路后,司机问:"去哪儿?"

海文把脸从膝盖上抬起,全身还在颤抖。"家。警察来告知我丈夫的不幸遭遇时,我想躺在床上。"

司机的目光在后视镜里与她的目光相遇,他的话没有留下任何误解的余地。"他们走后,你介意我为你遭受的损失慰藉一二吗?"

海文微微一笑,说:"我非常愿意。"

Black Veil

By Cassandra Jones

Haven Thornton-Mills stood in the obscure shadows outside the upscale Rosewood Resort, her refined features set in a stony mask as she watched her husband of twenty-seven years emerge through the extravagant brass doors with his latest whore draped across his arm. His boyish grin and swaggered stride left no doubt in Haven's mind what had just taken place behind closed doors. Brett embraced the woman who appeared half his age while the valet attendant brought his car around, a car which damn near cost Haven a fortune. Yet, the woman slid into the passenger's seat as if she owned the car and the man. Brett's despicable, profligate lifestyle had not only cost Haven money, it tarnished her name, left her pride bleeding like a wounded animal and self-confidence minuscule at best. But tonight, it was about to stop.

Drawing the mauve sweater around her slender shoulders to ward off the evening chill, Haven returned to the awaiting limo. Just as she settled into the soft leather seat with her long legs crossed and champagne in hand, the driver parted the center window. His golden gaze trailed appreciatively over her black dress and sheer hosiery. For a fleeting moment, she forgot Brett and his floozy, and allowed herself to indulge in a man's appreciation of her declining beauty. Although the tanned, muscular driver was much too young and she would never cross the line with employees, he still gave a boost to her libido, which she had declared legally dead.

"Follow him?" he asked.

Haven's lips stretched into a tight line. She simply nodded and set her gaze upon the resort's pristine property, its sloping, lush landscape and novelty shops quickly faded from view as the limo pursued Brett at a safe distance.

Prior to Brett's countless affairs, the black hole in Haven's heart had once been filled with endless love. Having been sheltered by her wealthy father, Wendell Thornton, and her inexperience with men, she was taken by Brett's deceitful charms the moment she'd gazed into his piercing green eyes. Within six months of meeting him and at the defiance of her father's wishes, they were married.

In a small town like New Lisbon, Wisconsin, rumors spread like wildfire, and it didn't take long to discover his insatiable taste in women and fine living. At Haven's expense, Brett carried on with his affairs, obtained three degrees from the best Universities in the world, and now at fifty-six, he still didn't know what he wanted to do with his life. What pained her most was his refusal to have children and now that her biological clock had long since taken its last tick, it would never happen. Through it all, she loved him.

However, tonight, as she looked ahead at the lover's silhouette under the night's sky, Haven only felt loathsome contempt for her husband. She imagined Brett between the woman's legs, foaming at the mouth, riding her like a dog in heat, oblivious of his sacred marital vows and the wife who'd given him everything. A renewed fury rose from the pit of her soul, blinding her with rage, consuming her with revenge. She hurled the champagne glass into the side window, shattering it to pieces. How dare he? Who the hell did he think he was?

"Is everything okay?" the smooth voice asked over the intercom.

Haven's insides shook so fiercely, she felt ill. Taking an unsteady breath, she retrieved her make-up compact from her purse and powdered her nose.

"Mrs. Mills?"

"I'm fine, just drive the damn car."

She reached out and took the bottle of champagne from the crushed ice, tilting it to her lips. The bubbly liquid swished around her mouth, the effects drifting to her head. She tilted the champagne for a second helping, but her entire body went still when the limo coasted to a stop on a dark, ominous street. She slowly set the bottle aside, her gaze followed Brett's car. Had her money been used to purchase this home? An iron gate parted, allowing him access to the impressive, well-kept property, nestled between collages of sugar maple trees. Brett parked in the circular driveway, climbed from the driver's seat and went to assist the woman out of the car. They giggled over a private joke and kissed passionately before he took her hand and disappeared through an arched entrance covered with climbing roses.

After what seemed like an eternity, Haven glanced at her diamond studded watch—only an hour had passed. She tugged at the blonde wig with gloved hands, making sure her chestnut hair didn't spill out.

It was time.

She pushed the limo's door open, stepped out and walked toward the residence. Her heels clicked softly against the cobblestone road. She pulled the gate and was pleasantly surprised to find it unlocked. Slipping through the small opening, she hurried to Brett's car and waited.

Fifteen minutes later, Brett finally strode out of the home, whistling. The closer he got, her heart grew heavy, knowing their life together would end tonight, and it weighed even more knowing he'd used her in every way possible.

Startled, Brett gasped and stepped backwards. "Haven, wha—what are you doing here?"

The wind carried the faint smell of a woman's perfume, considering it wasn't hers, Haven made the only sensible assumption. "I should be asking you the same question. What are you doing here?"

"I'm dropping off a friend. She was stranded…"

"Brett, don't insult my intelligence since we both know she's just another whore in your lifetime of lies."

He moved toward the car; his eyes blazed with anger. "We'll discuss this at home."

Haven's patience snapped. "You don't have a home. All you have is what's on your back and be thankful for that." She reached into her purse and extracted a paper and pen. "Sign," she said harshly.

He chuckled. "Do you really think I'm that stupid? It's going to take a lot to get rid of me. I'm used to a lucrative lifestyle and I expect it to continue whether we're together or not. So, go home where you belong. I'll meet you there."

"This is your last chance. Sign and I'll give you one hundred thousand dollars and a quiet divorce."

"You're pathetic. No other man will ever want you."

She had never detested him more. "You're right. To marry a loser like you, I am pathetic. As for another man, many are waiting to take your place, even the one you call your best friend." She placed the paper back in her purse. "My offer has expired."

Brett's face paled, his lips twisted into an evil snarl. "You're a dried up hag, Harold wouldn't have you."

"He already has." She turned on her heels and walked down the driveway. Although she'd lied about sleeping with Harold, the stunned look on Brett's face made up for the pain he so easily inflicted.

Brett called behind her. "This marriage has run its course. Besides, Carol and I want to be together. Two million dollars, I'll go away quietly." She did her best to ignore him, but hearing him refer to the other woman by name pierced her heart.

Haven returned to the limo, taking one last look over her shoulder at Brett as he got into his car. "Drive to the next block," she ordered the driver. Once they were in position, she removed a flat silver device from her purse. Her finger paused, contemplating her decision one last time. The humiliation, pain and anger, gave her the courage she needed. She pressed the button. A deafening explosion rocked the calm of the neighborhood as a ball of rumbling fire ripped through the sky, dispersing into multiple pockets of fire, thick smoke trailing in its wake. The ground beneath the limo vibrated; a street light flickered before casting them into total darkness. The limo sped forward.

After traveling a short distance, the driver asked, "Where to go?"

Haven lifted her face from her lap; tremors still ricocheted throughout her body. "Home. I want to be in bed when the police arrive to tell me of my husband's misfortune."

The driver's gaze met hers in the rearview mirror, and his words left no room for misunderstanding. "After they leave, would you mind me comforting you over your loss?"

Haven smiled. "I would like that very much."

一个小奇迹

汤姆·斯图希尔连着开了几个小时的车,突然内急要上厕所。已经是深夜了,他路过的所有加油站都关门了。随着时间一点点地过去,汤姆变得越来越绝望。最后,汤姆驱车驶下高速,来到沿路的第一个城镇。在那里,他拼命地寻找公厕。

汤姆继续驾着车,他现在内急得更厉害了,所以他加快了车速。正当他加速时,他听到有人用喇叭叫他把车停到路边。原来是这个镇的治安官,他走出他的车向着汤姆走去,他以威严的语气对汤姆说:"你觉得在这里应该以多快的速度行驶?"

"治安官,"汤姆道歉,"我从来没有开过这么快,但现在你也看到了,我亟须上厕所。"

治安官注意到汤姆语气中的真诚,对他表示同情。"我相信你沿着这条路走下去会找到厕所的,"治安官指着前面说,"但你要注意你的车速!"治安官补充道。

汤姆说:"我会的。"他如释重负,很高兴又能继续往前开了。

过了一会儿,汤姆看到前方一点亮光。他确定他马上要到24小时营业的便利店了,但越靠近目的地,前方的一座殡仪馆就越清晰。汤姆犹豫要不要用这里的厕所,但他太急着上厕所了,也就不考虑那么多了。他来到门口,停好车然后走了进去。

一进去,他就受到了热烈的欢迎,"欢迎,您愿意登记一下吗?"殡仪馆馆长吉福德先生问道。

"嗯……我来这仅仅是想借用您的厕所,"汤姆怀着歉意说道,"可以吗?"

"当然可以,"馆长回答道,"但是请先签一下名。"汤姆不明白为什么要签字,但还是按照要求签了,希望快点结束。汤姆正打算问男厕所在哪里的时候,突然吉福德先生说:"请再详细填写一下您的住址。"

汤姆带着困惑问道:"为什么需要我的住址呢?我到这里只是想用几分钟厕所而已。"

馆长回答道:"先生,请填写信息。"

汤姆一边写,一边嘴里嘟囔着:"真见鬼!"之后跟着吉福德先生进了男厕所。

在离开殡仪馆之前,汤姆出于对死者的尊重停留了一会儿。当汤姆走出殡仪馆以后,又一次看到了治安官,"谢谢你。"他对吉福德先生和治安官点了点头,于是,汤姆踏上了回家的路。

三个星期以后,汤姆接到了一个陌生男人的电话,他表明了自己律师的身份,他说:"三周前您在殡仪馆停留了几分钟用了厕所,我是律师,代表那场葬礼的主家,您需要在星期四的下午两点来我的办公室一趟。"

汤姆感到十分震惊,他惊慌失措地问道:"请告诉我,我犯了什么错吗?我是否需要一个律师?"

律师向他保证说,"不,没必要,准时到就可以了。"律师给汤姆留了一个地址后便挂了电话。

接下来的几天,汤姆都是在紧张不安中度过的。"我可能做什么事了?为什么他们给我打电话呢?"他自言自语,心里纳闷是怎么回事。

星期四，汤姆带着恐惧的心情按照律师的指示开车到了律师的办公室。他呼吸急促，心跳如捣，敲了敲前门。秘书说："请进。"律师走了出来，做了一个正式的自我介绍，然后领着汤姆进了办公室。汤姆惊讶地看到了治安官和殡仪馆的吉福德先生也在。

律师开始说："请坐，法院授权我来宣读斯坦·莫罗先生的遗嘱。"律师拿起汤姆曾签过字的客人名单，他转向殡仪馆馆长，指着汤姆问道："这是这个人签的字吗？"

"是的。"殡仪馆馆长说道。律师又看着汤姆说道："我猜你不认识莫罗先生，他很富有，镇上的大部分财富都归他所有。但是，他没有任何家人，人人都不喜欢他，实际上，镇上的人都躲避他。莫罗先生授权我做他的遗嘱执行人。"律师拿起文件接着说道："这是我曾起草的最短的遗嘱，只有如下这些内容：人人都讨厌我贪婪，我活着的时候没有人从我这里得到过一分钱。所以，显而易见，来我葬礼上的任何人都是出于对我这样的老傻瓜的同情，在此我所拥有的不动产和所有的私人财产都平分给那些参加我葬礼的人。"

接下来，律师直视着汤姆，"登记簿上唯一的签名是你的。"律师说道，"因此……"

世界有时残酷　但爱从未缺席

A Small Miracle

Tom Stonehill had been driving for several hours when he was overcome with the urge to go to the bathroom. It was late at night and all the gas stations he passed were closed. As time wore on, he became increasingly desperate. Finally, Tom exited the highway and drove into the first town along the road. There, he searched for a place that had facilities open to the public.

As he drove, his physical need took on heightened urgency and he started to pick up speed. Just as he began to accelerate, he heard someone on a loudspeaker instructing him to pull over to the side. It was the town sheriff. The sheriff got out of his car and approached Tom. "How fast do you think you can drive around here?" he asked in a formidable tone.

"Sir," apologized Tom, "I never drive this fast, but you see, right now I am in dire need of a bathroom."

The sheriff noted the sincerity in Tom's voice and took pity on him. "I believe there may be something open if you continue down this road," he said, pointing straight ahead. "But you gotta watch the speed limit!" he added.

"I will," replied Tom, relieved and glad to be moving on.

Moments later, Tom spotted a light in the distance. He was sure he was approaching a 24-hour-grocery store. But the closer he came to his destination, the more it became clear that he was headed toward a funeral parlor. Tom felt hesitant about using their facilities, but his urge was too strong to ignore. He drove up to the entrance, parked his car, and walked in.

Once inside, he was greeted warmly. "Welcome. Would you please sign in?" said Mr. Gifford, the funeral director.

"Uh...I'm just here to use the bathroom," Tom said apologetically. "May I?"

"Of course you may," responded the director, "but please sign in first." Tom couldn't figure out why it was necessary to write his name down, but he did as he was told and hoped that would end the matter. Tom was about to ask the whereabouts of the men's room when Mr. Gifford said, "Please write in your full address as well."

"But why do you need my address?" asked Tom, perplexed, "I'm just here to use the bathroom for a minute."

"Please, sir, fill in the information," came the reply.

"What the heck?" Tom muttered to himself as he wrote. Then he followed as Mr. Gifford led him to the men's room.

Before leaving the funeral parlor, Tom stopped for just a moment to pay his respects to the deceased. On his way out of the building, Tom saw the sheriff, "Thank you," he nodded to Mr. Gifford and the sheriff, and with that, Tom was off and on his way back home.

Three weeks later, Tom received a phone call from a man unknown to him, who identified himself as an attorney. "I represent the funeral home where you stopped to use the washroom a few weeks ago," the man said. "You need to be in my office this Thursday at 2: 00 p.m."

Tom was shaken. Alarmed, he asked, "Please tell me, did I do something wrong? Will I need a lawyer?"

"No, that won't be necessary." The attorney assured him. "Just be prompt," he said. The attorney gave Tom his address and then hung up the phone.

For the next few days, Tom was on edge. "What could I possibly have done? Why would they call me in?" he wondered aloud. That Thursday, he drove to the attorney's office with apprehension. Tom found the office building as instructed. With bated breath and a pounding heart, he knocked on the front door. "Come in," said the secretary. The attorney stepped out, formal introductions were made, and then Tom was directed to the office. Once inside, Tom was surprised to see both the sheriff and Mr. Gifford present.

"Please be seated," began the attorney. "I have been authorized by the court to read the last will and testament of Mr. Stanley

Murrow." The attorney picked up the guest book that Tom had signed. He turned to the funeral director, pointed at Tom and asked, "Is this the man who signed the book?"

"Yes," said the funeral director. Then the attorney looked at Tom and began, "I guess you didn't know Mr. Murrow. He was a very wealthy man. He owned most of this town. However, he did not have any family and was universally disliked, practically shunned by the townspeople. Mr. Murrow has authorized me to be his executor." The attorney picked up a document and continued. "This is the shortest will I have ever drawn up. It reads simply: Everyone hated my guts, and no one ever got any money from me when I was alive. So any person who comes to my funeral is obviously someone who had some compassion for an old coot like me. I hereby bequeath my entire estate with all my holdings to be divided equally among those who actually attended my funeral."

The attorney then looked straight at Tom. "Yours was the only signature that appeared in the register book," he said. "Therefore…"

维内诺上尉求婚

[西班牙]佩德罗·安东尼奥·德·阿拉克

"上帝啊！女人是个什么鬼啊！"上尉喊道，愤怒地跺着脚。"从我第一次见到她的时候，我就无缘无故地害怕她，为她而颤抖！我不再和她玩纸牌游戏，一定是命运的警告。这也是一个坏兆头，我度过了那么多不眠之夜。古往今来，哪一个人曾经像我现在这样迷茫？我爱她胜过爱我自己的生命，在她没有保护人时，我怎么能够把她一个人抛下？但是另一方面，我毕竟声明过反对婚姻，我又怎么娶她为妻呢？"

然后他转向奥古斯塔——"他们在酒吧里会怎么议论我？如果人们在街上看见一个女人挽着我胳膊，或者发现我在家中正在喂一个裹在襁褓中的孩子，他们会怎么议论我呢？我——能有孩子吗？为他们担惊受怕？永远生活在恐惧之中，担心他们生病或死亡？奥古斯塔，相信我，我们头上如果真有一位上帝的话，我是绝对不称职的！我要是这样做的话，用不了多久，你一定会被上帝召唤，或者离婚或者丧夫。听我的劝告：即使我向你求婚，也不要嫁给我。"

"你真是个奇怪的人，"年轻的女人气定神闲地说，腰板笔直地坐在椅子上。"所有这些都是你的自说自话！你凭什么断定我愿意嫁给你？我会接受你的求婚？虽然我不得不与许多跟我一样是孤儿的女孩儿一起日夜工作,我怎么会不喜欢一个人住?"

"我是怎么得出这个结论的呢?"上尉十分坦率地回答道,"因为不可能有别的结论。因为我们彼此相爱。因为我们互相吸引。因为像我这样的男人,像你这样的女人,不能有别的生活方式!你以为我不清楚吗?你以为我以前没有反思过吗?你以为我对你的美誉和名声漠不关心吗?我这样坦白是为了表明我的心意,为了从我的固有观念中解脱,为了测试我是否可以摆脱这进退维谷的可怕困境,它让我夜不能寐,为了尝试我是否能找到一个应急措施,这样我就不需要娶你——如果你决意孤独终老,我就会被迫无法娶你。"

"孤独终老!孤独终老!"奥古斯塔调皮地重复道。"那我为什么不找一个更有资格的终身伴侣呢?谁告诉过你,将来有一天我不会遇到一个我喜欢的人,一个不害怕娶我的人呢?"

"奥古斯塔!不要再说这个了!"上尉咆哮着,涨红了脸。

"为什么我们不能谈这个问题呢?"

"让我们不要提这个问题了,但是让我说,我要杀死那个敢向你求婚的人。但是就我来说,无缘无故地生气就是发疯。我不至于蠢到看不出我们俩的行为准则。要我告诉你吗?我们彼此相爱。别告诉我我错了!那是谎言。这就是证据:如果你不爱我,我也不会爱你!让我们各退一步吧。我要求延期十年。当我到年过半百的时候,当我作为年老体弱的老人,已经熟悉了奴隶制的概念,然后我们就瞒着众人结婚。我们会离开马德里,到乡下去,那里没有旁观者,那里没有人取笑我。但在这之前,请把我收入的一半偷偷拿走,不要让任何人知道。你继续住在这里,我继续住在我的房子里。我们会见到彼此,但只能在有旁人的情况下——例如,在社交场合。我们每天都会给对方写信。为了不损害你的美誉,我永远不会经过这条街,只有在阵亡将士纪念日那天,我们才会和罗莎一起去墓地。"

在善良的上尉的最后一次求婚之后,奥古斯塔忍不住莞尔一笑。但她的笑不是嘲笑,而是满足和快乐,就好像她的心中萌生了宝贵的希望,就好像她的天堂里升起了第一缕幸福的阳光!但是,作为一个女人——尽管像她们中间只有少数人勇敢,不会上当受骗——她还是设法抑制住了内心涌出的喜悦。她装出根本不抱希望的样子,带着一种疏离而冷淡的态度(这通常是真正的贞洁含蓄的特殊标志)说:

"你的特殊情况使你自己变得可笑。你定好了订婚戒指作为礼物,可是还没有人等你求婚呢。"

"我知道还有另一种方法——妥协,但这确实是不得已的下策。我来自亚拉贡的小姐,你全都明白了吗?那是下策,是同样来自亚拉贡的一位男人,求你给他讲解。"

她转过头来,直视着他的眼睛,带着一种说不出的热切、迷人、平静和充满期待的表情。

上尉从来没有见过她的容貌这样美丽,表情如此丰富;在他看来,她就像一位王后。

这个勇敢的士兵,这个赴汤蹈火、身经百战的男人,这个在枪林弹雨中冲锋陷阵如猛狮一般的男人,这个因此深深地打动了奥古斯塔的男人,此刻结结巴巴地说道:"奥古斯塔,请你给我这个荣幸,只有在一种确定无疑、完全必要、不容更改的情况下我才需要你的帮助。明天早上——今天——文件一准备好——越快越好。没有你我活不下去了!"

年轻姑娘的眼光变得温和了,她用温柔迷人的微笑来回报他坚定的英雄主义。

"但我再说一遍,只有一个条件。"勇敢的武士急忙重复了一遍,奥古斯塔的目光使他感到困惑和无力。

"什么条件？"年轻的姑娘问道，她把身子完全转过来，用她那双闪闪发亮的黑色明眸的魅力让他神魂颠倒。

"条件是，"他结结巴巴地说，"万一有了孩子，我们就把他们送到孤儿院去。我的意思是，在这一点上，我永远不会让步。你同意吗？看在上帝的分儿上，就答应了吧！"

"我为什么不答应呢，维内诺上尉？"奥古斯塔答道，伴随着一阵笑声。"你亲自把他们送过去，或者，更好的是，我们两个都去送。我们会毅然决然地放弃他们，既不亲吻他们，也没有其他动作！你不认为我们应该一起把他们送到那里去吗？"

奥古斯塔一面这么说着，一面用极度喜悦的目光看着上尉。上尉觉得自己都要幸福死了，不禁泪如雨下。他把面色绯红的女孩拥入怀中，说道："这么说我迷失了？"

"无可救药地迷失了，维内诺上尉。"奥古斯塔答道。

1852年5月的一个早晨，也就是在这刚刚描述的一幕四年之后，我的一个好朋友给我讲了这样一个故事。他骑着马停在位于马德里旧金山大道的一座宅邸外，他把缰绳扔给马夫，问在门口迎接他的那个穿长衣的男仆："你的主人在家吗？"

"劳驾您上楼去，他在书房里。主人不喜欢通报他有人来访。每个人都可以直接去找他。"

"幸亏我对这座房子了如指掌。"这位陌生人一面上楼梯，一面自言自语地说。"在书房！好吧，好吧，谁会想到维内诺上尉竟会喜欢科学呢？"

客人在房间里踱来踱去，又遇见一个仆人，仆人又重复了一遍："主人在书房里。"最后，他走到仆人们所说的那间屋子的门口，迅速地打开门，他停住了脚步，在面前的这组奇人奇景面前，惊奇得差不多石化了。

在房间的中央,地板的毯子上,一个男人正在爬行。一个小男孩,大约一岁半的样子,站在那人的头的前面,显然一直在抓他的乱发。另一个大约三岁的小男孩骑在他的背上,用脚后跟踢着他的两侧,小家伙一只手抓住父亲的领巾,使劲儿地拉着,把领巾当成了缰绳,用孩子那特有的、快活的声音高兴地喊道:"驾!毛驴儿!驾!"

Captain Veneno's Proposal of Marriage

By Pedro Antonio de Alarcón

"Great heavens! What a woman!" cried the captain, and stamped with fury. "Not without reason have I been trembling and in fear of her from the first time I saw her! It must have been a warning of fate that I stopped playing *écarté* with her. It was also a bad omen that I passed so many sleepless nights. Was there ever mortal in a worse perplexity than I am? How can I leave her alone without a protector, loving her, as I do, more than my own life? And, on the other hand, how can I marry her, after all my declaimings against marriage?"

Then turning to Augustias— "What would they say of me in the club? What would people say of me, if they met me in the street with a woman on my arm, or if they found me at home, just about to feed a child in swaddling clothes? I—to have children? To worry about them? To live in eternal fear that they might fall sick or die? Augustias, believe me, as true as there is a God above us, I am absolutely unfit for it! I should behave in such a way that after a short while you would call upon heaven either to be divorced or to become a widow. Listen to my advice: do not marry me, even if I ask you."

"What a strange creature you are," said the young woman, without allowing herself to be at all discomposed, and sitting very erect in her chair. "All that you are only telling to yourself! From what do you conclude that I wish to be married to you; that I would accept your offer, and that I should not prefer living by myself, even if I had to work day and night, as so many girls do who are orphans?"

"How do I come to that conclusion?" answered the captain with the greatest candor. "Because it cannot be otherwise. Because we love each other. Because we are drawn to each other. Because a man such as I, and a woman such as you, cannot live in any other way! Do you suppose I do not understand that? Don't you suppose I have reflected on it before now? Do you think I am indifferent in your good name and reputation? I have spoken plainly in order to speak, in order to fly from my own conviction, in order to examine whether I can escape from this terrible dilemma which is robbing me of my sleep, and whether I can possibly find an expedient so that I need not marry you—to do which I shall finally be compelled, if you stand by your resolve to make your way alone!"

"Alone! Alone!" repeated Augustias, roguishly. "And why not with a worthier companion? Who tells you that I shall not some day meet a man whom I like, and who is not afraid to marry me?"

"Augustias! Let us skip that!" growled the captain, his face turning scarlet.

"And why should we not talk about it?"

"Let us pass over that, and let me say, at the same time, that I will murder the man who dares to ask for your hand. But it is madness on my part to be angry without any reason. I am not so dull as not to see how we two stand. Shall I tell you? We love each other. Do not tell me I am mistaken! That would be lying. And here is the proof: if you did not love me, I, too, should not love you! Let us try to meet one another halfway. I ask for a delay of ten years. When I shall have completed my half century, and when, a feeble old man, I shall have become familiar with the idea of slavery, then we will marry without anyone knowing about it. We will leave Madrid, and go to the country, where we shall have no spectators, where there will be nobody to make fun of me. But until this happens, please take half of my income secretly, and without any human soul ever knowing anything about it. You continue to live here, and I remain in my house. We will see each other, but only in the presence of witnesses—for instance, in society. We will write to each other every day. So as not to endanger your good name, I will never pass through this street, and on Memorial Day only we will go to the cemetery together with Rosa."

Augustias could not but smile at the last proposal of the good captain, and her smile was not mocking, but contented and happy, as if some cherished hope had dawned in her heart, as if it were the first ray of the sun of happiness which was about to rise in her heaven! But being a woman—though as brave and free from artifices as few of them—she yet managed to subdue the signs of joy rising within her. She acted as if she cherished not the slightest hope, and said with a distant coolness which is usually the special and genuine sign of chaste reserve:

"You make yourself ridiculous with your peculiar conditions. You stipulate for the gift of an engagement-ring, for which nobody has yet asked you."

"I know still another way out—for a compromise, but that is really the last one. Do you fully understand, my young lady from Aragon? It is the last way out, which a man, also from Aragon, begs leave to explain to you."

She turned her head and looked straight into his eyes, with an expression indescribably earnest, captivating, quiet, and full of expectation.

The captain had never seen her features so beautiful and expressive; at that moment she looked to him like a queen.

"Augustias," said, or rather stammered, this brave soldier, who had been under fire a hundred times, and who had made such a deep impression on the young girl through his charging under a rain of bullets like a lion, "I have the honor to ask for your hand on one certain, essential, unchangeable condition. Tomorrow morning—today—as soon as the papers are in order—as quickly as possible. I can live without you no longer!"

The glances of the young girl became milder, and she rewarded him for his decided heroism with a tender and bewitching smile.

"But I repeat that it is on one condition," the bold warrior hastened to repeat, feeling that Augustias's glances made him confused and weak.

"On what condition?" asked the young girl, turning fully round, and now holding him under the witchery of her sparkling black eyes.

"On the condition," he stammered, "that, in case we have children, we send them to the orphanage. I mean—on this point I will never yield. Well, do you consent? For heaven's sake, say yes!"

"Why should I not consent to it, Captain Veneno?" answered Augustias, with a peal of laughter. "You shall take them there yourself, or, better still, we both of us will take them there. And we will give them up without kissing them, or anything else! Don't you think we shall take them there?"

Thus spoke Augustias, and looked at the captain with exquisite joy in her eyes. The good captain thought he would die of happiness; a flood of tears burst from his eyes; he folded the blushing girl in his arms, and said: "So I am lost?"

"Irretrievably lost, Captain Veneno," answered Augustias.

One morning in May, 1852—that is, four years after the scene just described—a friend of mine, who told me this story, stopped his horse in front of a mansion on San Francisco Avenue, in Madrid; he threw the reins to his groom, and asked the long-coated footman who met him at the door: "Is your master at home?"

"If your honor will be good enough to walk upstairs, you will find him in the library. His excellency does not like to have visitors announced. Everybody can go up to him directly."

"Fortunately I know the house thoroughly," said the stranger to himself, while he mounted the stairs. "In the library! Well, well, who would have thought of Captain Veneno ever taking to the sciences?"

Wandering through the rooms, the visitor met another servant, who repeated, "The master is in the library." And at last he came to the door of the room in question, opened it quickly, and stood, almost turned to stone for astonishment, before the remarkable group which it offered to his view.

In the middle of the room, on the carpet which covered the floor, a man was crawling on all-fours. On his back rode a little fellow about three years old, who was kicking the man's sides with his heels. Another small boy, who might have been a year and a half old, stood in front of the man's head, and had evidently been tumbling his hair. One hand held the father's neckerchief, and the little fellow was tugging at it as if it had been a halter, shouting with delight in his merry child's voice: "Gee up, donkey! Gee up!"

衬衫夫人的回忆

衬衫夫人已经与约翰逊家族一起生活了三代。这对一件衣服来说可不是寻常业绩。她经历了岁月的洗礼，虽然有些褪色，料子也磨薄了，但她还是受到这家一代又一代人的宠爱。

衬衫夫人永远也不会忘记与约翰逊曾祖母第一次见面的那一天。当时她被挂在衣架上，曾祖母对她一见钟情！曾祖母把她拿到光亮处，边笑边大声说："这件衬衫真是太完美了，我要永远跟她在一起。"

但善良的老曾祖母说话不算话。在年复一年穿着她参加花园聚会和海滩野餐以后，曾祖母把她传给了她的女儿约翰逊奶奶。至此，开启了艰难岁月。约翰逊奶奶对衬衫夫人的特殊宠爱使得其他衣服妒火中烧。裙子小姐和围巾夫人对她尤其刻薄，后来她们甚至挑拨内衣小姐与衬衫夫人反目成仇！

约翰逊奶奶常在一些特殊场合穿衬衫夫人，衬衫夫人则把这视为遭到其他衣服嘲笑的鼓励。事实上，每当心情沮丧的时候，她都会回忆一下往事：在初春首日跟约翰逊奶奶一起去公园里散步；一起喂养刚出生的小宝宝；还有一起在厨房里烤饼干的美妙时光！

今天，衬衫夫人将会被传给家族里的另一位成员！她既兴奋又紧张：约翰逊夫人，还有她现有的那些衣服会如何待她？

让她大喜过望的是，新衣服们都张开双臂接受了她！她发现有些衣服已经跟这家一起生活了整整五代了,比如高曾祖父的冬大衣!他们一拍即合,很快就开始交流昔日那些美好时光里的故事!其他衣服则在一旁如饥似渴地听着。欢乐在新季节一定会旧日重现!

Mrs. Blouse's Memories

Mrs. Blouse had been with the Johnson family for three generations. This was no mean feat for an article of clothing. She had survived the test of time; and though her colors were faded and her material worn thin, she was still loved through and through.

Mrs. Blouse could never forget the day when Great Grandma Johnson had first discovered her on the clothing rack—it was love at first sight! Great Grandma had held her up to the light and laughed as she exclaimed, "This is the perfect blouse; I'll never part with it."

Well, good old Great Grandma hadn't quite lived up to her word. After years of garden parties and beach picnics Great Grandma had passed Mrs. Blouse on to her daughter, Grandma Johnson. This was the beginning of a difficult season. The special attention that Grandma Johnson gave her made the other clothing jealous! Ms. Skirt and Mrs. Scarf were particularly mean towards her. Eventually, they even managed to turn Ms. Undergarment against her!

Grandma Johnson often wore Mrs. Blouse on special occasions;

this was an encouragement for Mrs. Blouse in light of all the ridicule she endured. In fact, whenever Mrs. Blouse was feeling depressed she would turn to her memories: walking through the park with Grandma Johnson on the first day of spring, feeding the new baby together, or just baking cookies in the kitchen.

Today Mrs. Blouse was again being passed on to another family member! Mrs. Blouse was both excited and nervous—how would Mrs. Johnson and her current clothing treat her?

Much to her delight, the new clothes accepted her with open arms! She discovered that some articles of clothing had been with the family for five generations—Great, Great Grandpa's winter coat! They hit it off together and were soon swapping stories of the good old days. The other garments listened eagerly. This new season would bring joy once more!

黑洞之旅

[美国] 汤姆·马赫尼

他们沿着小溪远足,意外地发现峡谷一侧的崖壁上有一个石灰岩洞。

"咱们进去看看吧。"他说。

她皱起了眉。"我不想去。"

"来吧,就看一眼。"

他从双肩包里拿出手电筒,走进了洞穴。她很不情愿,也只好勉强地跟他走了进去。洞里凉爽却有霉味,地面既平滑也有坑洼。蝙蝠在手电筒的光柱里飞速掠过,水滴不时地从洞穴顶上滴滴答答地落下来。他们继续往纵深走去,直到抵达一个三岔路口。

"好了,咱们看过了,"她说。"回去吧。"

他看了看左边的那个分洞,说:"再往里走一点。"

她用脚尖在泥里标出一个箭头,指示他们的返程路线,然后跟了上去。这个岩洞有很多分洞和隧道。在每一个转折处,她都做了标记,但是返程之旅也变得越来越复杂了。他走得很快,她尽力紧跟才能跟得上。

"等一下。"她说。

他不耐烦地停了下来:"怎么了?"
"你想找什么呀?"
"我不知道。"
"这里有些瘆人,咱们回去吧。"
"再等几分钟。"

他转过一个弯继续向前走,却被绊倒了。手电筒脱了手,在地上翻滚,跌进了一个石灰岩的岩缝里。洞穴里立刻变得黑乎乎的,寂静无声。他跪下来,伸手去摸手电筒,但没摸到。

"真倒霉。"他说道。
"你没带火柴吗?"
"没带。咱们贴着墙往回走吧。"

他们一点一点地往前挪,墙上沾满了蝙蝠的粪便。在黑暗中,很难判断距离。他们走了很长时间,感觉就像是在绕圈子一样。两人心里都不由得恐慌起来。

"咱们得停下。"她说。
"我觉得快到入口了。"
"咱们要迷路了,给我一分钟,让我想清楚。"

他不情愿地停了下来。

"我觉得咱们应该已经到了第一个分叉那里,"她说,"你觉得呢?"

他不置可否地耸了耸肩。

"最近你总是做事不计后果。好像你什么都不在乎似的。"

他嘟囔着:"咱们还是好好想想怎么出去吧。"

他们在狭窄的走廊里摸索着走了很长时间,通道渐渐宽阔,出现了一个分叉。他们不知道该走哪条路,只好颓靠在湿冷的石灰岩上,听着岩洞顶上的水滴答滴答落下来的声音,还有他们气喘吁吁的呼吸声。

黑暗的环境让人忐忑不安,产生幽闭恐惧。

几个小时过去了。她能闻到他身上的汗臭味,想起他最近隐隐约约表现出的逃避,这种逃避是他对她冷漠的表现,这勾起了她的火。

"要是咱们活着出去,你得多洗碗。"她说。

这话在黑暗中听起来突兀怪异。他转向她,这是一个下意识的动作。黑暗里什么也看不见,但是他能够想象出她那熟悉的表情:皱着眉头,额头扭曲,蓝色的眼睛里充满敌意。

"什么?"他问。

"洗碗,"她说,"我不愿意跟在你后面打扫了。"

他厌倦了她的唠叨。"草坪不是我打理的吗?你从来都不尊重我为此付出的劳动。"

"如果你尊重我为打扫卫生所付出的劳动,我就会尊重你为草坪所付出的劳动。"

"体味问题不是我能控制的,都是因为饮食,你做饭时蒜放得太多啦!"

"洗澡是他们的新发明吗?"

"让我像你那样一天洗十遍脚?你有强迫症!"

"我素来讨厌你妈,"她喊道,"她把我当废物。但是我从来没说过。你一次都没替我说过话。"

"她素来也不喜欢你。她还不想让我娶你呢。但是我没有听。我还总是护着你。看来是我错了!"

接下来,他们陷入了沉默。岩洞里只有滴答滴答的声音。

一天过去了,两天过去了。他们尝试了几次,都是徒劳的。食物耗尽了,水也没了,喉咙渴得难受。现在,连洞顶滴水的地方都找不到了。他们都懒得说话,各揣心腹事,渐渐陷入了绝望之中。

她怀疑跟他在一起是不是在浪费生命。他怀疑自己结婚是不是太早。他们都困惑于如果幸存下来，两人的关系会不会发生变化。无论是继续还是结束，情况必然都和以前不同了。

时间流逝，他们的身体越来越虚弱，对对方也越来越绝望了。

"让咱们最后试一次。"她说。

他垂头丧气，都不想说话了，只是点点头。

他们用最后的力量沿着通道缓慢地行进。大约过了一小时，他们停了下来。

"算了吧，"他说，"咱们永远出不去了。"

恐惧感在两人间传递，他们无能为力，他们执着的那些鸡毛蒜皮，已成定局。或许到了放弃的时候了。为什么？是因为厌倦，还是幽闭产生的轻蔑？现在似乎都不重要了。

"听。"她说。

"什么？"

"嘘。听到了吗？是水声。"

"咱们一直能听到水滴的声音啊。"

"不是水滴，是水流。我想那是溪水的声音。咱们一定已经到了入口附近了。咱们接着走。"

他们沿着墙壁前进，直到一道微弱的光刺破了黑暗。他们跌跌撞撞地向阳光奔去，出现在阳光下。松树的味道扑面而来，阳光刺眼。他们站在那里，不敢相信这是真的，眯眼看着眼前的风景，眯着眼睛面面相觑。黑洞抹掉了一层否认，隐藏的真相又暴露在了阳光之下。

微笑浮上了她的嘴角。他摸着僵硬的脖子，报以放声大笑。他们步履艰难地走向轿车，开车回家了。

那一夜他洗了碗，她只洗了一次脚。两人没有吵架，而是相依而眠,甜蜜地进入梦乡。

哪位哲人说过,有时候,婚姻就是一场互相携手的旅行。在这场黑洞之旅中,谁又不是在磕磕绊绊中行进呢?

The Cave

By Tom Mahony

They hiked along a creek and stumbled upon a limestone cave tucked into the canyon wall.

"Let's check it out," he said.

She frowned. "I don't know."

"C'mon, just a peek."

He removed a flashlight from his backpack and entered the cave. She protested, but grudgingly followed him inside. It was cool and musty, the ground slick and rutted. Bats darted through the flashlight beam, water dripped from the ceiling. They walked down a corridor until it branched in three directions.

"Okay, we've seen it," she said. "Let's turn around."

He started down the left corridor. "Just a little further."

She toed an arrow in the mud to mark their return path, and followed. The cave splintered into numerous caverns and tunnels. At each junction she marked their path but the return route became increasingly complicated. He walked faster. She struggled to keep pace.

"Wait," she said.

He stopped, impatient. "What?"

"What are you looking for?"

"I don't know."

"This is getting spooky. Let's go back."

"A few more minutes."

As he turned to continue, he stumbled. The flashlight flew from his hands, rolled across the floor, and disappeared down a fissure in the limestone. The cave went black, silent. He dropped to his knees, searching in vain for the flashlight.

"Shit," he said.

"Do you have any matches?"

"No. Let's follow the walls back to the entrance."

They inched forward, the walls gooey with bat guano. Distance was difficult to judge in the darkness. They walked a long time. It felt like they were going in circles. They fought panic.

"We need to stop," she said.

"I think we're getting close."

"We're just getting lost. Let's think it through for a minute."

He reluctantly stopped.

"I knew we should've turned back at that first junction," she said. "What were you thinking?"

He shrugged.

"You've been doing so many reckless things lately. Like you don't care what happens to you, to us."

He grunted. "Let's just focus on getting out of here."

They shuffled down the narrow corridor until it widened and forked. They had no idea where to go. They slumped against the cold damp limestone, listening to the drip, drip, drip of water from the ceiling, the steady labor of their breathing. The intensity of the darkness was unnerving, claustrophobic.

Hours passed. She could smell the sweat on him, that vague funk he'd acquired of late, a symbol of his indifference. Something about that triggered her fury.

"If we survive this, you need to do the dishes more," she said.

The words sounded bizarre in the darkness. He turned to her, a pointless move; there was nothing to see. But he could picture her face: that familiar frown, scrunched forehead, hostile blue eyes.

"What?" he asked.

"The dishes," she said. "I'm tired of cleaning up after you."

He was sick of her nagging. "What about my lawn care? You've never respected the effort that's gone into it."

"I will, if you respect the importance of hygiene."

"I can't control my body odor. It's a diet thing. I eat a lot of garlic."

"They invented this new thing called a shower."

"Should I wash my feet ten times a day like you do? It's

borderline compulsive."

"I've always hated your mother," she said, almost yelling. "She treats me like crap. But I can't say anything to her. You need to stand up to her for once."

"She never liked you either. She warned me not to marry you, but I've always defended you. Always. Maybe I was wrong."

They went silent. Drip, drip, drip.

A day passed, two. Several more forays through the cave proved futile. Their food and water ran out, throats raging with thirst. They couldn't find the source of the dripping water. They barely spoke, drifting into their respective states of despair.

She wondered if she'd wasted her life with him. He wondered if he'd married too young. They both wondered how their relationship would change if they survived. It would either flourish or die, but it couldn't stay the same.

They grew weaker and more despondent with each hour.

"Let's give it one last shot," she said.

He nodded, too dejected to speak.

They gathered their strength and crept down the corridor. After perhaps an hour, they stopped.

"Forget it," he said. "We'll never make it out of here."

An awful dread passed between them, a finality about things they could've done differently, the trivialities they'd obsessed on. Why? Boredom? Pent up contempt? Didn't matter now.

"Listen," she said.

"What?"

"Shh. Hear that? It's water."

"We've heard dripping water the whole time."

"Not dripping, flowing. I think it's the creek. We must be near the entrance. Let's keep going."

They followed the walls until a faint glow broke the darkness. They stumbled toward it and emerged in daylight. The smell of pine was overwhelming, the glare punishing. They stood in disbelief, squinting out over the landscape, squinting at each other. The cave had scrubbed away a layer of denial, a hidden truth exposed in sunlight.

A smile spread across her lips. He rubbed his neck and managed a laugh. They trudged to the car and drove home.

He did the dishes that night. She washed her feet only once. The two did not quarrel, but in each other's arms in their sweet dreams.

An philosopher said that marriage is, sometimes, a journey of hand in hand with each other. In this trip of black caves, no one is not stumbling.

大大的惊喜

她的生活就这样被两句话毁了。她现在知道了,当她低头盯着手机屏幕时,手机屏幕似乎故意在回视她。她不得不把这些字读了好几遍,才敢相信是真的。

"你把我的事告诉你妻子了吗?我什么时候能再见到你?"

当爱丽丝站在餐桌旁拿着丈夫的手机时,她惊讶地发现自己没有任何感觉,没有怒火,没有忐忑,甚至没有一丝痛苦。她的整个身体似乎被瞬间速冻了,大概是为了保护她不至于崩溃吧。但是她的心里却再清楚明白不过了,她知道,丈夫出轨了。

她以前也曾怀疑过哪里有点不对头,但不是那种性质的。最近,他举止反常,虽然变化不是很大,但足以告诉她,他的生活中发生了一些她不知道的事情。因为她没有弄清楚他到底有什么不同,去质问他什么问题,她的理由还不够充分。她太清楚了,这样的谈话是不会有结果的。

她的丈夫汤姆是那种人,不愿把自己内心最深处的想法和感受告诉别人,甚至对他的妻子也是如此。他曾经对她说过,他很自豪能把最重要的事留给自己,她不应该试图改变这一点。在他们的整个婚姻过程中,她明白了他有真情,同时他也真心希望她远离任何不愉快的事情。虽然她知道,一个比妻子大十岁的丈夫这样做也算合情合理,但她从来没有能够完全接受这种性格。一方面,这是一种居高临下的态度;另一方面,这样有意隐瞒对他们的婚姻是有害的。现在果然出事了。

"爱丽丝!"一个低沉的声音突然喊道。原来是汤姆冲进浴室,不慎划伤了一根手指。通常他都不让她见血。就在那时,爱丽丝拿起了他放在厨房桌上的手机,偷看了他的信息。她以前从来没有这样做过,但是在过去的几个星期里,她注意到他身上发生了一些细微的变化,把她的好奇心吊到了极致,到了无法克制的地步。

"爱丽丝?"他又喊了一声。

"是啊,怎么回事?"她把他的手机放回桌上,她努力让自己的声音听起来很随意,手机放的位置和角度跟原来分毫不差。

"我们把绷带放在哪儿了?我找不着了。"

爱丽丝迟疑了几秒钟,没有回答。当一个妻子发现她的丈夫即将为了另一个女人离她而去的时候,她对丈夫说什么合适呢?她自问。"在最上面的架子上。"她大声回答。

当左手食指缠着绷带的汤姆出现在厨房时,爱丽丝禁不住认为这是因果报应,是对他的惩罚。他那棕色的眼睛望着她,脸上带着她一向喜爱的那种微笑,嘴角弯弯的。"我想你是对的,"他说,"我切胡萝卜切得太快了。"他从桌上拿起手机看了看,好像在查看有没有新信息。

"我通常都是对的,不是吗?"爱丽丝一边说,一边仔细观察他脸上的表情。那张脸上没有透露出任何蛛丝马迹。

汤姆拉过一把椅子坐下,眼睛仍然紧盯着他的手机。他叹了口气。"有件事我应该告诉你……"

爱丽丝能感觉到心在怦怦直跳。当他告诉她,他们将近十五年的婚姻已经结束时,她会做何反应?她会精神崩溃放声大哭吗?还是勃然大怒?她怎么能知道呢,因为这种情况对她来说是完全陌生的,她从来没有和除汤姆以外的人约会过，分手这种事情，她只从别人的嘴里、杂志上的文章和电视报道听说过。"听起来很有趣。"她说，声音微微有些颤抖。她想大喊，我们的孩子，卢卡斯和艾米怎么办？你想过他们吗？

"呃，是这样的，"汤姆从手机上抬起头，直视着她的眼睛。"我好像有个女儿，但我对她并不了解……"

"是女儿吗？"爱丽丝气喘吁吁地说。这就是那个信息的相关内容吗？

"是的，很明显。"汤姆摇摇头。"我认识她妈妈是在多年以前，在我遇见你很久以前认识的。现在我女儿找到了我，想了解我。她想见见卢卡斯和艾米。我想邀请她来我们家，但前提是先征得你的同意……"

汤姆记得接下来爱丽丝紧紧地抱着他，抱得他几乎透不过气来。"你当然可以邀请她来！太棒了！太棒了！"她喜极而泣。

A Big Surprise

Two sentences, that's how much it took to shatter her life. She knew that now as she was gazing down on the cell phone screen that seemed to be intentionally glaring back at her. She had had to read the words several times to suspend her disbelief.

"Have you told your wife about me? When can I see you again?"

Alice was surprised that she didn't feel anything, not anger or panic or even a hint of pain, as she stood next to the kitchen table with her husband's phone in her hand. It was as if her whole being had instantly frozen up on the inside, perhaps to protect her from falling apart. But in her mind there was perfect clarity. She knew that her husband was having an affair.

She had suspected that something was wrong, but not that. Lately his demeanor had changed, not a lot, but enough to tell her that something was going on in his life that she did not know about. Because she had not been able to put a finger on what exactly was different about him. she hadn't had a good reason to ask him what was going on. She knew all too well that such conversation would go nowhere.

Tom, her husband, was not one to share his innermost thoughts and feelings with others, even his wife. He had told her once that he took pride in keeping his concerns to himself, and that she shouldn't try to change that. All through their marriage she had learned that he really meant it, and that he had a genuine desire to keep her away from anything unpleasant. Although she knew that this could be expected from a husband who was ten years older than his wife, she had never been able to fully reconcile herself with this trait. On the one hand it was condescending, and on the other it was secretive and poisonous to their marriage. And now this had happened.

"Alice!" a muffled voice suddenly called. It came from the bathroom where Tom had rushed in after having cut himself on a finger. Typically him he wanted to spare her of the sight of blood. It was then that Alice had picked up his cell phone, which he had left on the kitchen table, and had looked at his messages. She had never done that before, but the little changes she had noticed in him over the last few weeks or so had driven her curiosity to a point where she no longer could contain it.

"Alice?" he called again.

"Yeah, what is it?" She tried to sound casual as she put his phone back on the table, in exactly the same place and position as it had been before.

"Where do we keep the bandages? I can't find them."

For a few seconds Alice hesitated to answer. What would be the appropriate thing for a wife to say to her husband when she has just found out that he is going to leave her for another woman? she asked herself. "On the top shelf", she called back.

When Tom reemerged in the kitchen with a bandage on his left index finger Alice couldn't help thinking that it was Karma that had punished him. He looked at her with his brown eyes and the same crooked smile that she had always loved. "Guess you were right", he said, "I was cutting those carrots too fast." He took up his phone from the table and looked at it, as if checking for new messages.

"I'm usually right, ain't I?" Alice said while she carefully studied the expression on his face. It didn't reveal anything.

Tom pulled out a chair and sat down, with his eyes still fixed on his phone. He sighed. "There is something I should tell you…"

Alice could feel her heart pounding. How would she react when he told her that their almost fifteen years long marriage was over? Was she going to break down crying? Or would she fly into a rage? How could she know when this kind of a situation was completely new to her? As she had never even dated any other than Tom, breakups were something she only knew from other people, from magazines and television. "Sounds interesting," she said with a slight trembling in her voice. She wanted to yell what about Lucas and Amy, our kids, have you thought about them?

"Well, it is." Tom looked up from his phone and straight into her eyes. "It seems that I have a daughter I didn't know about…"

"A daughter?" Alice gasped. Was that what the message was about?

"Yes, apparently." Tom shook his head. "I knew her mother many years ago, long before I met you. Now she has tracked me down, and wants to get to know me. And she wants to meet Lucas and Amy. I would like to invite her to our house, but only as long as you are OK with it…"

The next thing Tom knew was Alice holding her arms around him so tight that he almost couldn't breathe. "Of course you can! That's wonderful! Wonderful!" she sobbed.

校园霸凌者

[美国]罗杰·迪安·凯泽

我走进佐治亚州布伦瑞克市的哈德餐厅,所有的座位都坐满了,于是我坐在吧台上。我拿起餐单,看着各式各样的菜名想着我是吃早饭呢还是直接吃午饭。

"不好意思。"有人拍了下我的肩膀说道。

我抬起头转过身去,看见一位长得还挺好看的女士站在我身后。

"你叫罗杰吧?"她问我。

"是啊。"我回答道,不禁面露困惑,因为我之前根本没见过这个女人。

"我叫芭芭拉,我丈夫叫托尼。"她说道,用手指了指远处通向卫生间门旁边的一张桌子。

我顺着她手指的方向看去,只见那里有个男人独自坐在桌边,我不认识。

"对不起。我,呃,我有点糊涂了。我想我不认识你俩。不过。我确实叫罗杰,罗杰·凯泽。"我告诉她。

"他叫托尼·克莱斯顿。佛罗里达州杰克逊维尔兰登高中的托尼啊,想起来了?"她问道。

"真对不起。我对这个名字没什么印象。"我说道。

她转身回到她的餐桌坐了下来。我看见她随即跟她丈夫说起话来,还时不时地在座位上回过头来直勾勾地看着我。

我最后决定点份早餐和一杯无咖啡因咖啡。我坐在那一直绞尽脑汁地想这到底是哪个托尼。

"我肯定认识他。"我心中暗想。"他肯定是因为什么原因认出了我。"我端起咖啡抿了一口。突然,我灵机一动,想了起来。

"托尼,校园霸凌者托尼。"我咕哝着,坐在凳子上转过身去,面朝他所在的方向望去。

"我上七年级地理课时遇到的那个校园霸凌者。"我想。

有多少次,这个糟糕的家伙当着全班女生的面取笑我的大耳朵?有多少次,这个糟糕的狗娘养的嘲笑我没有父母、住在孤儿院?有多少次,这个校园大霸凌为了让其他同学觉得他是一个大人物,把我推到走廊的储物柜上?

他举起手来向我挥了挥。我笑笑,也朝他挥挥手作答,然后转过身来吃我的早饭。

"天哪。他现在好瘦,完全不是我1957年记忆中的那个大块头家伙了。"我心想着。

突然我听到盘子碎了的声音,于是我转过身来想看看发生了什么。托尼在试图坐上轮椅时,不小心把桌子上的几个盘子碰掉了。他们吃饭的时候,轮椅就停在通往卫生间的过道上。服务员跑过去捡摔碎了的盘子,我听见托尼和他妻子忙不迭地道歉。

托尼的妻子推着轮椅上的托尼经过我身边,我抬起头笑了笑。

"罗杰。"他边说边点头。

"托尼。"我也点头作为回应。

我看着他们出了门，慢慢走向一辆大货车，车的侧门有一架轮椅装卸器。

我坐在那看着他妻子一遍又一遍地试着把活动坡道放下来，可一直放不下来。最后，我起身结了账，向货车走去。

"有什么问题吗？"我问道。

"可恶的棍子卡在轮子里了。"托尼说。"你能帮我把他弄到车上去吗？"他妻子问道。

"我觉得我能行。"我说道，边接过轮椅边把托尼推到副驾驶车门前。我打开了车门，锁上了轮椅上的刹车。

"好的，伙计，现在抱紧我的脖子。"我边说边伸手搂住他的腰，小心地把他抬到货车副驾驶座位上。

当托尼松开我脖子的时候，我伸手把他那没有知觉的双腿一条一条地放进车里，这样就正好固定在他面前了。

"你都记得，是吗？"他说道，直视着我的眼睛。

"托尼，我记得。"我说。

"我猜你一定会想，'真是恶有恶报'。"他说道，声若游丝。

"我绝对不会这么想，托尼。"我说道，一脸严肃。

他伸出手来握住我的双手，紧紧地握着。

"我现在坐轮椅的感觉和你当初住在孤儿院的感觉一样吧？"他问我。

"差不多吧，托尼。不过，你很幸运，你身边有爱你的人可以推着你四处走走看看。我当年身边却没有人爱我。"我回答。

我从口袋里掏出印着电话号码的名片递给了他。

"有空就打电话给我。我们可以约个午饭。"我告诉他。我俩一起哈哈大笑起来。

  我站在那看他们朝洲际公路开去,最终消失在南行的坡道处。我希望他有空的时候能打电话给我。那他就是我高中时代唯一的朋友了。

The Bully

By Roger Dean Kiser

I walked into the Huddle House restaurant in Brunswick, Georgia and sat down at the counter as all of the booths were taken. I picked up a menu and began to look at the various items trying to decide if I wanted to order breakfast or just go ahead and eat lunch.

"Excuse me," said someone, touched me on the shoulder.

I looked up and turned to the side to see a rather nice looking woman standing before me.

"Is your name Roger by any chance?" she asked me.

"Yes." I responded, looking rather confused as I had never seen the woman before.

"My name is Barbara and my husband is Tony," she said, pointing to a distant table near the door leading into the bathrooms.

I looked in the direction that she was pointing but I did not recognize the man who was sitting, alone at the table.

"I'm sorry. I'm, ah. I'm ah, confused. I don't think that I

know you guys. But my name is Roger. Roger Kiser," I told her.

"Tony Claxton. Tony from Landon High School in Jacksonville, Florida?" she asked me.

"I'm really sorry. The name doesn't ring a bell." I said.

She turned and walked back to her table and sat down. She and her husband immediately began talking and once in a while I would see her turn around in her seat and look directly at me.

I finally decided to order breakfast and a cup of decaffeinated coffee. I sat there continually racking my brain trying to remember who this Tony guy was.

"I must know him," I thought to myself. "He recognizes me for some reason." I picked up my coffee up and took a sip. All of a sudden it came to me like a flash of lighting.

"Tony. TONY THE BULL." I mumbled, as I swung myself around on my stool and faced in his direction.

"The bully of my seventh grade geography class," I thought.

How many times that sorry guy had made fun of my big ears in front of the girls in my class? How many times this sorry son-of-a-gun had laughed at me because I had no parents and had to live in an orphanage? How many times this big bully slammed me up against the lockers in the hallway just to make himself look like a big man to all the other students?

He raised his hand and waved at me. I smiled, returned the wave and turned back around and began to eat my breakfast.

"Jesus. He's so thin now. Not the big bulky guy that I remember from back in 1957," I thought to myself.

All of a sudden I heard the sound of dishes breaking so I spun around to see what had happened. Tony had accidentally hit several plates knocking them off the table as he was trying to get into his wheelchair which had been parked in the bathroom hallway while they were eating. The waitress ran over and started picking up the broken dishes and I listened as Tony and his wife tried to apologize.

As Tony rolled by me, being pushed by his wife, I looked up and I smiled.

"Roger," he said, as he nodded his head forward.

"Tony," I responded, as I nodded my head, in return.

I watched as they went out of the door and slowly made their way to a large van which had a wheelchair loader located in the side door of the vehicle.

I sat and watched as his wife tried, over and over, to get the ramp to come down. But it just would not work. Finally I got up, paid for my meal, and I walked up to the van.

"What's the problem?" I asked.

"Darn thing sticks once in a while," said Tony. "Could you help me get him in the van?" asked his wife.

"I think I can do that," I said as I grabbed the wheelchair and rolled Tony over to the passenger door. I opened the door and locked the brakes on the wheelchair.

"OK. Arms around the neck Dude," I said as I reached down and grabbed him around the waist and carefully raised him up into the passenger seat of the van.

As Tony let go of my neck I reached over and swung his limp, lifeless legs, one at a time, into the van so that they would be stationed directly in front of him.

"You remember. Don't you?" he said, looking directly into my eyes.

"I remember, Tony," I said.

"I guess you're thinking, 'What goes around comes around'," he said, softly.

"I would never think like that, Tony," I said, with a stern look on my face.

He reached over and grabbed both of my hands and squeezed them tightly.

"Is how I feel in this wheelchair how you felt way back then when you lived in the orphan home?" he asked me.

"Almost, Tony. You are very lucky. You have someone to push you around who loves you. I didn't have anyone." I responded.

I reached in my pocket and pulled out one of my cards that had my home telephone number written on it and I handed it to him.

"Give me a call sometimes. We'll do lunch," I told him. We

both laughed.

I stood there watching as they drove toward the interstate and finally disappeared onto the southbound ramp. I hope he calls me sometime. He will be the only friend that I have from my high school days.

回家的感觉真好

一阵微风吹过詹妮弗的头发。金红色的太阳即将落山。她坐在海滩上,望着那团火红的圆球,不禁惊异于它的颜色:中间是深红的,向外柔柔地淡成黄色。她只能听到海浪的声音,还有在天空中那高高飞翔的海鸥的声音。

眼前的美景使她放松下来,出走几天以后,她感到这才是她所需要的。她想:"天色已晚,我该回家了,父母会惦记我去哪里了。"她在猜测自己离家出走三天以后回来,父母会有什么反应。她一直走着,径直走向163号小屋,每年暑假,她都是在那里度过的。路上空空荡荡的,没有人,她慢慢地、悄无声息地走着,再有几百米就能安全到家了。

此时,天色确实完全黑了下来,几分钟前太阳落了山,天气也越来越冷了。她真希望自己穿着那件她最喜欢的卫衣,那该有多暖和啊!她想象着卫衣正穿在自己身上呢。可是一看见她家的前门,这种想法就烟消云散了。眼前的一切有些异样。外面的花园好几天没人侍弄的样子,她大吃一惊:她父亲平时做事一板一眼的,所有东西都保持干净整洁,而现在呢……花园好像被废弃了。她不明白出了什么事。

她进了屋,先进了厨房,看见父亲留的一张字条,上面写着:"亲爱的埃伦,这是煮好的咖啡,我出去找找。"埃伦就是她母亲的名字,但是——母亲在哪儿呢?走廊的右边是她父母的卧室,她走进去就看见了母亲,她躺在床上睡着了。母亲看起来是那么疲惫,好像好几天没睡过觉的样子,面色异常苍白。詹妮弗真想把她叫醒,但是母亲看起来太累了,真不忍心叫醒她。于是詹妮弗也躺在她身旁睡了。詹妮弗醒来时发现有些异样:她不在母亲的房间里了,穿的也不是离家出走时的旧衣服了。她是穿着睡衣躺在自己惬意的床上。

回家的感觉真好啊。忽然她听见一个声音:"亲爱的,你现在感觉好点了吧?你知道吗?你把我们吓死啦!"

Being Back Home

A gentle breeze blew through Jennifer's hair. The golden red sun was setting. She was on the beach, looking up at the fiery ball. She was amazed by its color, deep red in the middle, softly fading into yellow. She could hear nothing but the waves and the seagulls flying up above in the sky.

The atmosphere relaxed her. After all she had been through, this is what she needed. "It's getting late," she thought, "I must go home, my parents will be wondering where I am." She wondered how her parents would react, when she got homer the three days she was missing. She kept on walking, directing herself to bungalow 163, where she spent every summer holiday. The road was deserted. She walked slowly and silently. Just in a few hundred meters she would have been safe in her house.

It was really getting dark now, the sun had set a few minutes before and it was getting cold too. She wished she had her favorite Jumper on it kept her really warm. She imagined having it with her. This thought dissipated when she finally saw her front door. It seemed different. Nobody had taken care of the outside garden for a few days. She was shocked: her father was usually so strict about keeping everything clean and tidy, and now…It all seemed deserted. She couldn't understand what was going on.

She entered the house. First, she went into the kitchen where she saw a note written by her father. It said: "Dear Ellen, there is some coffee ready, I went looking." Ellen was her mother but-where was she? On the right side of the hallway was her parents' room. She went in. Then she saw her. Her mother, lying on the bed, sleeping. Her face looked so tired, as if she hadn't slept for days. She was really pale. Jennifer would have wanted to wake her up but she looked too tired to force her. So Jennifer just fell asleep beside her. When Jennifer woke up something was different… she wasn't in her mother's room and she wasn't wearing the old clothes she ran away in. She was in her cozy bed in her pajamas.

It felt so good being back home. Suddenly she heard a voice. "Are you feeling better now, dear? You know you got us very, very scared."

他的青春期就这样结束了

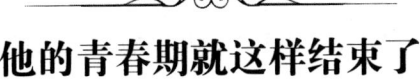

［加拿大］莫利·卡拉汉

晚上了,药店快要关门了。年轻的阿尔弗雷德·希金森在这家药店工作,这时候他正穿上自己的外套准备回家。他走向药店门时,经过萨姆·卡尔先生身旁。卡尔先生个子身材瘦小,头发灰白,是这家药店的老板。当阿尔弗雷德经过的时候,卡尔先生看着他的后背,用非常轻柔的声音说道:"走前请等一会儿,阿尔弗雷德,就一会儿。"

卡尔先生的声音非常轻柔,让阿尔弗雷德感到不安。

"什么事?卡尔先生。"

"在你离开药店前,请你最好把口袋里的几样东西拿出来留在这里。"卡尔先生说。

"什么东西!你在说什么呀?"阿尔弗雷德说。

"阿尔弗雷德,你口袋里有一盒粉饼、一管口红,还有一组套装牙刷。"

"你什么意思?"阿尔弗雷德回答他说。"你觉得我是疯了吗?"他的脸不由得红了。

卡尔先生继续冷冷地看着阿尔弗雷德,阿尔弗雷德不知道该说什么,只是眼睛尽量躲避着他的老板。

过了一会儿，他把手伸进口袋，拿出偷的那些东西。

卡尔先生说："就是这些东西，请你最好说出这种事你干了多长时间了。"

"这是我第一次拿东西。"

卡尔先生快速回应道："所以现在你觉得你编瞎话就骗得了我，你觉得我看起来像傻瓜吗？我不知道店里面发生了什么事情吗？我告诉你，你干这事已经有很长时间了。"

卡尔先生的脸上浮现出奇怪的笑容。

他说："我不想叫警察，但是我可以打电话给你父亲，让他知道我要把你送进监狱。"

"我父亲不在家，他是印刷工，上夜班。"

"那谁在家？"卡尔先生问。

"我想我妈妈会在家。"

卡尔先生盯着他走向电话，由于恐惧，阿尔弗雷德的嗓门提高了，他想摆出一副天不怕地不怕的样子，他每次惹是生非以后都如此。自从离开学校后，这样的事情频发，每次他都会像今晚一样大声说话。

他对卡尔先生说："请等一会儿，你不必把其他人也牵涉进来，你不用告诉我妈。"阿尔弗雷德尽量让自己听起来像个大人，然而在内心深处他还是个孩子，他希望家里人可以快点赶过来救他。但是卡尔先生已经跟他妈妈通上话了，告诉她赶快到药店来一趟。

阿尔弗雷德想象着他妈妈可能会冲进来，愤怒的眼睛像要喷火。他想向她解释时，她可能会大喊大叫，一把推开他，也许会让他觉得特别自惭形秽。尽管如此，他现在只想让妈妈快点过来，赶在卡尔先生叫警察来之前。阿尔弗雷德和卡尔先生都在默默地等，终于他们听见有人来到紧闭的门前。卡尔先生打开门，脸绷着，表情严肃地说："请进，希金森夫人。"

阿尔弗雷德的妈妈面带友好的微笑走进来，主动向卡尔先生伸出手来，彬彬有礼地说道："我是希金森夫人，阿尔弗雷德的妈妈。"

卡尔先生惊讶于希金森夫人进来时所表现出的风度，她镇定自若、安静平和，十分友好。

希金森夫人问："阿尔弗雷德又惹事了吗？"

"他确实闯祸了，他一直在从店里偷东西，拿了像牙膏、口红这种可以轻易出手转卖的小商品。"

希金森夫人看着她的儿子难过地说："阿尔弗雷德，是这样吗？"

"是的。"

"你为什么要这么干？"她问。

"我把钱花在我认为该花的地方上了。"

"花在什么上了？"

"就是和小伙伴们一起四处逛逛，我想。"阿尔弗雷德说。

希金森夫人伸出手，用漂亮的指甲温和地碰了碰卡尔先生的胳膊，好像她了解卡尔先生的感受，好像她不想再给他造成更多的麻烦，她说："在你采取行动之前，能不能请你先听我说说。"她的声音听起来很冷静，还把头偏了偏，好像她已经说得够多了一样。然后她带着和蔼可亲的微笑再次看着卡尔先生说："卡尔先生，您想怎么处理呢？"

"我想给警察打电话叫辆警车，这是我应该做的。"

她回答："是的，我也觉得应该这么做。不能因为他是我的儿子就救他，不过有时我又觉得对于一个处在生命懵懂时期的男孩来说，一个有益的小建议也许是对他最有效的教育。"

对于儿子的这些叛逆行为，希金森夫人的应对方式与众不同。她带着温和的笑容说："不知你是否认为让他跟我回家不太好，因为他看起来像一个大男孩，不是吗？"

有好一会儿，大家都在思考这个问题。

卡尔先生原本以为阿尔弗雷德的妈妈会焦虑不安地走进来，吓得浑身发抖，含泪乞求宽恕她的儿子。但是她没有，她泰然自若，和蔼可亲。这反倒让卡尔先生觉得有些内疚，片刻过后，卡尔先生和她握了手，表示同意她的想法。

他说："当然了，我不会这么冷酷，我会告诉你我会怎么做，告诉你的儿子别再来药店，然后这件事情就不予追究了，就像现在这样。"接着他热情地和希金森夫人握了握手。

"我永远不会忘记你的善意！"

"不好意思，"卡尔先生说，"我们这次用这样的方式认识，但很高兴与你接洽，就为了让他改邪归正，仅此而已。"

"最好以后再不要像这样见面了，不是吗？"她说。

他们俩突然拉着彼此的手，好像他们很喜欢彼此，好像已经认识了很久。

"那么晚安，先生？"

"晚安，希金森夫人，真的很抱歉这样。"

妈妈和儿子离开了药店，走在街上，默默无语。希金森夫人迈着大步子，直视前方。过了一会儿，阿尔弗雷德说："谢天谢地，以后再也不要有这种情况发生了。"

"安静！不要和我说话，你已经让我够丢人了！这会儿就懂事点，安静！"

他们终于走到家了。希金森夫人脱掉外套，甚至没有看阿尔弗雷德一眼，就对他说："你真倒霉，还好上帝宽恕了你！麻烦事一件接一件，总是惹是生非！傻乎乎站在那干吗？上床睡觉去。"

她一边往厨房走,一边说:"今晚发生的事情,一个字也不要对你爸提起。"

　　阿尔弗雷德躺在床上,听着母亲在厨房里的动静,内心却毫无愧疚,只是为母亲今天的强势而骄傲。他对自己说:"她真镇定。"他觉得一定要告诉妈妈,她今天多么了不起。当他走进厨房的时候,他看见母亲正在喝茶,看到眼前的这一幕,他无比震惊。据他说,他母亲的脸上满脸惊恐和疲惫,跟之前在药店里的那一副泰然自若、满面春风的样子判若两人。希金森夫人双手颤抖地拿起茶杯,一些茶都溅在了桌子上,她的嘴唇紧张地颤抖着,看起来非常苍老。他默默地看着妈妈。妈妈这个样子让他想哭,他觉得自己的青春期就这样结束了。他意识到过去他给妈妈带来的所有麻烦,让妈妈双手颤抖,让她担惊受怕,灰白的脸上留下了深深的皱纹。这似乎是他第一次真正了解他的妈妈。

His Youth Came to an End

By Morley Callaghan

The drug store was beginning to close for the night. Young Alfred Higgins who worked in the store was putting on his coat getting ready to go home. On his way out, he passed Mr. Sam Carl, the little grey-hair man who owned the store. Mr. Carl looked up at Alfred's back as he passed, and said in a very soft voice, "Just a moment, Alfred, one moment before you go."

Mr. Carl spoke so quietly that it worried Alfred.

"What is it? Mr. Carl."

"Maybe you will be good enough to take a few things out of your pockets and leave them here before you go." said Mr. Carl.

"What things? What are you talking about?"

"You've got a compact and a lipstick and a list two-two of toothpaste in your pockets, Alfred."

"What do you mean?" Alfred answered, "Do you think I'm crazy?" his face got red.

Mr. Carl kept looking at Alfred coldly. Alfred did not know

what to say and tried to keep his eyes from meeting the eyes of his boss.

After a few moments he put his hand into his pockets and took out the things he had stolen.

"That is things, Alfred." said Mr. Carl, "and maybe you will be good enough to tell me how long this has been going on."

"This is the first time that I ever took anything."

Mr. Carl was quick to answer, "So now you think you tell me a lie? What kind of food do I look like? I don't know what goes on in my own store. I tell you, you've been doing this for a long time."

Mr. Carl had a strange smile on his face.

"I don't like to call the police," he said, "but maybe I should call your father and let him know I'm going to have to put you in jail."

"My father is not home, he is a printer. He works nights."

"Who is at home?" Mr. Carl asked.

"My mother, I think."

Mr. Carl stared to go to the phone. Alfred's fears made him raise his voice. He wanted to show he was afraid of nobody. He acted this way every time he got into trouble. This had happened many times since he left school. At such times he always spoke in a loud voice as he did tonight.

"Just a minute." he said to Mr. Carl, "You don't have to get anybody else into this. You don't have to tell her." Alfred tried to sound big. But deep down he was like a child. He hoped that someone at home would come quickly to save him. But Mr. Carl was already talking to his mother. He told her to come to the store in a hurry.

Alfred thought his mother would come rushing in, eyes burning with anger. Maybe she would be crying and would push him away when he tried to explain to her. She would make him feel so small. Yet, he wanted her to come quickly before Mr. Carl called in a policeman. Alfred and Mr. Carl waited but said nothing. At last they heard someone at the closed door. Mr. Carl opened it and said, "Come in, Mrs. Higgins." His face was hard and serious.

Alfred's mother came in with a friendly smile on her face and put out her hand to Mr. Carl and said politely. "I'm Mrs. Higgins, Alfred's mother."

Mr. Carl was surprised at the way she came in. She was very calm, quiet and friendly.

"Is Alfred in trouble?" Mrs. Higgins asked.

"He is. He has been taking things from the store, little things like toothpaste and lipsticks. Things he can easily sell."

Mrs. Higgins looked at her son and said sadly. "Is it so? Alfred."

"Yes."

"Why have you been doing this?" she asked.

"I've been spending money I believe."

"On what?"

"Going around with the boys, I guess." said Alfred.

Mrs. Higgins put out her hand and touched Mr. Carl's arm with great gentle nails as if she knew just how he felt. She spoke as if she did not want to cause him any more trouble. She said, "If you will just listen to me before doing anything." Her voice was cool and she turned her head away as if she had said too much already. Then she looked again at Mr. Carl with a pleasant smile and asked, "What do you want to do, Mr. Carl?"

"I was going to get a car. This was I should do, call the police."

She answered, "Yes, I think so. It's not for me to save because he is my son. Yet I sometimes think a little good advice is the best thing for a boy at soaking times in his life."

Mrs. Higgins looked like a different woman to her son outspread, there she was with a gentle smile saying, "I wonder if you don't think it would be better just to let him come home with me. He looks like a big fellow, doesn't he?"

Yet it takes some of the long time to get any senses into their heads.

Mr. Carl had expected Alfred's mother to come in nervously, shaking with fear, asking with wet eyes for mercy for her son. But no, she was most calm and pleasant. And was making Mr. Carl feel guilty. After a time, Mr. Carl was shaking his head in agreement with what she was seeing.

"And of course." he said, "I don't want to be cool. I will tell you what I'll do. Tell your son not to come back here again. And let it go at back. Now was that." And he warmly shook Mrs. Higgins' hand.

"I will never forget your kindness."

"Sorry we have to meet this way." said Mr. Carl, "but I am glad I got in touch with you. Just want him to do the right thing. That it is all."

"It's better to meet like this than never, isn't it?" she said.

Suddenly they held hands as if they liked each other, as if they had known each other for a long time.

"Good night, sir?"

"Good night, Mrs. Higgins. I'm truly sorry."

Mother and son left. They walked along the street in silence. She took long steps and looked straight in front of her. After a time, Alfred said, "Thank God it turn out to like that never again."

"Be quiet! Don't speak to me, you have shamed me enough! Have the decency to be quiet."

They reached home at last. Mrs. Higgins took off her coat and without even looking at him, she said to Alfred, "You are a bad luck. God forgive you! It's one thing after another. Always have them. Why do you stand there so stupidly? Go to bed!"

As she went into kitchen, she said, "Not a word about tonight to your father."

In his bedroom, Alfred heard his mother in the kitchen. There was no shame in him, just pride in his mother's strength. "She was smooth." he said to himself. He felt he must tell her how great she was. As he got to the kitchen he saw his mother drinking a cup of tea. He was shocked by what he saw. His mother's face as he said was a frightened, broken face. It was not the same cool bright face he saw earlier in the drug store. As Mrs. Higgins lifted the teacup her hands shook. And some of the tea splashed on the table. Her lips moved nervously. She looked very old. He watched his mother without making a sound. The picture of his mother made him want to cry. He felt his youth come into an end. He saw all the troubles he brought his mother in her shaking hand, in the deep lines of worry in her grey face. It seemed to him that this was the first time he had ever really seen his mother.

她留下了她的鞋

她留下了她的鞋子,其他的她统统都带走了——包括她的牙刷、她的衣服,甚至我们摆放在桌子上装糖果的银色小花瓶,她直接把糖果倒在桌子上,然后把瓶子拿走了。这个二人世界的小蜗居看上去已经和以前不大一样了,属于她的东西虽然原本也不是很多,可都给搬得干干净净,这间房子现在就如同一个智力拼板玩具,还有几块残缺,不复完整。衣柜也基本空空如也,反正里面的东西本来都是她的。然而就在衣柜的底层,也像往常一样堆放着的,是她留下来的鞋子,一只也不少,她为什么要把鞋子留下来呢?她绝对不可能是忘拿的,我知道她向来为她买的鞋子而得意。可是,这些鞋子真的就放在那里,还包括那双黑色的凉鞋,她的至爱凉鞋——宽宽的鞋面,上面还镂刻有花纹图,鞋底已经磨损破旧,她的脚趾印还依稀可见。

这可真让我百思不得其解,她走出了我的生活,却没有带走她的鞋子,这是一种讽刺吗?还是我想歪了?从某种角度说,我又暗自高兴,鞋子既然给留下来了,那么她总有一天会回来拿的,对吗?我的意思是说没了这些鞋子,她以后日子怎么过啊?可是,她不会再回来了,我知道她不会的,她宁愿光脚踩玻璃也不愿意回来看我和她所有鞋子的。可是,老天!她怎么就把鞋子给留下来呢?所有的鞋,包括每一双球鞋、靴子、凉鞋、高跟鞋、木屐、人字拖……我该怎么办呢?让它们放在这儿，还是打包扔到垃圾箱里？我是不是要每天打开衣柜就看见它们，然后冥思苦想她留下鞋子的目的呢？她一定是故意这么做的，她很清楚自己在做什么。这些鞋子我不能扔掉，因为我怕有一天她会回来拿。她的鞋就这样依旧留在我的生命里，彻底摆脱对她的思恋是不可能的，无论是鞋子还是鞋子的主人我都无法舍弃。

她的鞋子在我心中留下的深深印迹实在难以抹去，我只能痴痴地看着她的鞋子，看着这些鞋带、绑带、纽扣和花纹，它们依旧将我和她连在一起，虽然方式是那样遥远和滑稽可笑。回想起我们在一起的美好时光，想着她在那时那刻穿着哪双鞋。鞋子是她的，不是别人的，是她把鞋跟磨短了，鞋边磨破了，鞋内是她的纤纤足印。我坐在地板上，坐在她的这些鞋子旁边，想着她穿着这些鞋子到过多少地方，走过多少路？她最后下定决心要离开我的时候穿的又是哪双鞋呢？我拿起了一只她常穿的高跟鞋，心不在焉地嗅一下，我一点也不觉得恶心，因为我所能拥有的、实实在在的、能让我感知到的、与她的联系就只剩那味道了。她把鞋子留了下来，把其他的东西都带走了，只留下了鞋子，它们躺在我衣柜的底层，那个对她专属回忆的圣地神龛。

She Left Her Shoes

She left her shoes: she took everything else—her toothbrush, her clothes, and even that stupid little silver vase on the table we kept candies in. Just dumped them out on the table and took the vase. The tiny apartment we shared seemed different now: her stuff was gone. It wasn't much really, although now the room seemed like a jigsaw puzzle with a few pieces missing incomplete. The closet seemed empty too most of it was her stuff anyway. But there they were at the bottom, piled up like they usually were, every single one of them, Why did she leave her shoes? She could have forgotten them, I knew too well that she took great pride in her shoe collection, but there they still were, right down to her favorite pair of sandals. They were black with a design etched into the wide band that stretched across the top of them, the soles scuffed and worn, a delicate imprint of where her toes rested was visible in the soft fabric.

It seemed funny to me she walked out of my life without her shoes. Is that irony or am thinking of something else? In a way I was glad they were still here, she would have to come back for them, right? I mean how could she go on with the rest of her life without her shoes? But she's not coming back, I know she isn't. She would rather walk barefoot over glass than have to see me all of her shoes! All of them. every sneaker, boot and sandal, every high heel and clog, every flip-flops. What do I do? Do I leave them here or bag them up and throw thorn in a trash? Do I look at them every morning when I get dressed and wonder by she left them? She knew what she's doing. I can't throw them out for fear she may return for them today. I can't be rid of myself of her completely with all her shoes still in my life, can't dispose of them or the person that walked in them.

Her shoes left deep foot print up my heart, and I can't sweep it away. All I can do is stare at them and wonder, stare at their laces and straps, their buttons and tread. They still connect me to her though, in come distant bizarre way. I can't remember the good times we had, which pair she was wearing at that moment in time. They are hers and no one else's. She wore down the heels, and she scuffed their sides, it's her fragile foot paint imbedded on the insole. I sit on the floor next to them and wonder how many places had she gone while wearing these shots, how many miles had she walked in them, which pair was she wearing when she decided to leave me? I pick up a high heel she often wore and absently smell it. I don't think it is disgusting. It's just the last tangible link I have to her, the last bit of reality I have of her. She left her shoes; she took everything else except her shots. They remain at the bottom of my closet, a shrine to the memory about her.

援助之手

[美国] 科雷斯顿·福尔曼

马特坐在沙发上,看着电视屏幕里的人物在他眼前晃来晃去,让他最难忘的却是卡罗尔的笑。她的笑声很特别,每次都会让他忍俊不禁。

他正在看的这部电影是一部喜剧电影,里面有卡罗尔最喜欢的演员。他知道如果她还在,肯定会笑得前仰后合。但他也会跟着笑得前仰后合。

但是事实上她不在。整个客厅空荡荡的,没有笑声。

她去世快两年了,尽管卡罗尔停止呼吸之前一直坚决要求他续弦,找个新伴侣共同生活,他却没有这个意向。

他为什么要这么做?马特经常自问。他已经有两个女儿,女儿们也都各自成了家,他还有了三个可爱的外孙。他们都住得很近,只要马特想见到他们就可以见到。

有时在家,也会有为数不多的几个小时,他会有孤独感,但他要学会适应这种孤独感。他工作,与朋友在一起,足以占满他空闲的时间。

另外,如果他的两个女儿,亚历山德拉和帕特丽夏有了继母,她们会有什么感觉?她们和他说过希望他再找个伴儿,但他不确定她们说的是不是真话。因为她们才是他的全部。

他所需要的一切都应有尽有,只是失去了欢声笑语。

电话响了,马特接起在他旁边的咖啡桌上的电话。她想要我帮什么忙吧?马特看到显示屏上显示是帕特丽夏打来的。她是两姐妹中的妹妹,自从嫁了世界上最不务实的丈夫迈克尔,每当有东西坏了,她就习惯性地给她父亲打电话。今天是礼拜六,马特想,显而易见,她是有什么实际问题需要他帮忙解决。

"我是爸爸。"他接起电话。

"嗨,爸爸,"帕特丽夏的声音从另一头传来,像往常一样,请爸爸来帮忙时,声音怯怯的。"今天忙吗?"

"不忙,但是希望你今天是有别的事。"

"我需要你帮帮我。我的一个同事送给我们一张桌子,但我们的小汽车实在放不下。你能开卡车去她家吗?可能还要再带一个工具箱把桌子卸下来。"

半小时后,马特把他的皮卡货车开进了帕特丽夏指定地址的车道上。和他预想的一样,帕特丽夏站在门外门廊的车道上等着他,一看到他就朝他挥了挥手。在她旁边一个女人倚墙而立。她比帕特丽夏高些,深褐色的短发。看起来50岁左右,和他岁数差不多。马特想,这就是帕特丽夏慷慨的同事吧。

"你好,我是马特。"他说着握了握那个女人的手。

"我叫丽萨。"那个女人答道,不好意思地笑着,褐色的明眸一闪,流露出真诚的善意。"帕特丽夏大概告诉你了,我是她的同事。她告诉我正想在客厅里放一个桌子,我立刻告诉她我正要处理这张旧的,要买张新的。"

"我看这个桌子也很新啊。"帕特丽夏说,亲热地看着丽萨。"我也这么认为。她在工作时把什么东西都保护得很好,所以她用过的家具也会保护得很好。"

他女儿在他面前对那个女人赞不绝口,马特本能地细细打量起她来。他想,她看起来也还不错。实际上,她是一个大美人。"好了,只要它不在你吃饭的时候散了架就好,不得不说你赚了。"

"的确,从帕特丽夏告诉我她丈夫有多能吃,桌子的承受力就是个问题了。"丽萨哈哈大笑。马特随即也哈哈大笑起来。

并不是因为想到迈克尔的饭量让他哈哈大笑,而是丽萨的笑声让他哈哈大笑。丽萨的笑声像极了卡罗尔,他想。他向帕特丽夏瞥了一眼,注意到了帕特丽夏心照不宣地微微一笑。

她已经把我给出卖了?他正疑惑着看向她女儿,他知道女儿会明白他什么意思。帕特丽夏笑得更开心了,这就是给他的答案。

"马特,我只向帕特丽夏提了一个小要求来换走这张桌子,"丽萨看着马特,目光里有恳求。"就是想借她父亲来帮我安装一下新桌子。"

"当然可以,"马特回答。"我很乐意!"他说的是实话。

A Helping Hand

By Kresten Forsman

It was her laughter that he missed the most, Matt realized as he sat on the couch and watched the images that flickered on the television screen in front of him. Carol had had this special laugh that had never failed to make him also laugh.

The movie he was watching was a comedy and had one of Carol's favorite actors in it. He knew that she would have been laughing very hard if she had been there. And he would have too.

But she wasn't there. And the living room was completely empty of laughter.

It had already been almost two years since she had passed away and although Carol had insisted until her last breath that he should move on and try to find someone else to share his life with, he had no intention of doing so.

Why would he? Matt had often asked himself. He still had his two daughters and their families, which included three lovely grandchildren. And they all lived close by and he could see them as often as he wanted.

Those few hours of loneliness he felt when he was at home, he would learn to cope with. His work and his friends would be enough to keep his thoughts occupied.

And besides, how would Alexandra and Patricia, his two daughters, feel about getting a stepmother? They had both told him that they were hoping that he would start looking for someone, but he wasn't sure if they really meant it. And they meant everything to him.

He had everything he needed. It was only the laughter he was missing.

His phone rang and Matt picked it up from the coffee table next to him. She wants my help with something, Matt thought as he saw the name Patricia on the screen. She was the younger of the two and since her husband, Michael, was not the most practical man in the world, she had the habit of calling her dad whenever she needed something fixed. This being Saturday, Matt thought, made it even more obvious that she needed his help with some practical matter.

"This is Dad," he said as he answered.

"Hi, Dad," Patricia's voice said at the other end, sounding a little timid as she usually did when she was about to ask for his help. "Are you very busy today?"

"No, but I expect that you are about to change that."

"I need your help with something. One of my colleagues has offered me a table for free, but it's too big for our car. Could you bring your truck to her place, and maybe a tool box for disassembling the table?"

Half an hour later Matt pulled into the driveway with his pickup at the address Patricia had given him. As he had expected, Patricia was standing on the driveway porch outside the front door, waving at him as soon as she saw him. Next to her a woman was leaning against the wall. She was taller than Patricia and had short dark-brown hair. She looked to be around fifty, like himself. Patricia's generous colleague, Matt figured.

"Hi, I'm Matt," he said as he shook the woman's hand.

"I'm Lisa," the woman answered, smiling insecurely as a sparkle in her brown eyes revealed a genuine kindness. "As Patricia probably has told you, I am one of her co-workers. When she told me that she was looking for a table for their living room, I told her immediately that I am about to get rid of mine, because I'm getting a new one."

"The table I'm getting looks brand new," Patricia said, looking affectionately at Lisa. "But I expected that. She takes so good care of everything at work, so I knew her furniture would all be in pristine condition."

His daughter's praise of the woman in front of him, made Matt instinctively study her. She didn't look bad, he thought. Actually, she was quite a looker. "Well, as long as it won't collapse while you're eating, I'd say you've got a pretty good deal."

"Actually, from what Patricia has told me about how much her husband eats, that could become a problem." Lisa laughed. And immediately Matt started laughing too.

It wasn't thinking of Michael's eating habits that made him laugh, but Lisa's laughter itself. Just like with Carol, he thought. When he glanced at Patricia, he noticed her knowing smile.

Has she set me up? he thought as he gave his daughter an asking look, knowing that she would understand. Patricia's widening smile was his answer.

"Matt, I asked Patricia for only one small favor in return for this table," Lisa said as she looked at Matt with a begging look in her eyes. "That I would be able to borrow her dad to help me assemble my new table."

"Of course," Matt answered. "I'd be happy to!" And he meant it.

碧波倒影里的爱情

[意大利] 威廉·施文克·吉尔伯特

我是一个可怜的瘫子,已经瘫痪多年,活动范围仅限于一张床或一张沙发。近六年以来,我孤身一人蜗居在一间小屋内,小屋朝向威尼斯城的一侧有一条运河,只有一个耳聋的老太太照顾我的日常饮食起居。我将自己临摹的花卉、水果的水彩画(这也是威尼斯最便宜的临摹对象了)寄给我在伦敦的一个朋友,托他卖给一个画商换大约30英镑的微薄的收入,这笔小钱精打细算也只够维持一年的生活。但是,总的来说,我还是快快乐乐、心满意足的。

我有必要详细地描述一下我所在房间的位置:这个房间只有一扇窗户,距离下面的支流河面五英尺(1.5米),而在窗户之上,房子伸出河面上大约有六英尺(1.8米)长,伸出那部分用结实的木桩支撑,木桩打入运河的河床里。这样的布局带来了一个不便(还有其他不便),那就是限制了我仰视的视野,只能看到正对面房子十英尺(3米)高以下的部分;然而,虽然身体残疾,但是若尽我所能,对于窗下这条不足15英尺(4.5米)宽的运河,我还是可以看见运河上下相当长一段距离内的风景。但是,虽然我不能一览对面房子的全貌,却可以看见其在运河里的倒影,房内的住户不时地在阳台或窗户上显露身影(总是上下颠倒的），这一颠倒的倒影让我兴致盎然。

　　当六年前我刚搬入这间屋子的时候，就注意到了一个约莫13岁的小姑娘（我尽力猜测的）的倒影，她每天都会在阳台上出没，而这个阳台却正巧超出我的视野范围。每当天气晴好的时候，从早到晚，她都会一直坐在那里辛勤劳作，座位之侧摆放着一张小桌子，桌子上放着一瓶花和一个十字架，据我的推断，她靠做针线活谋生。如果我没有猜错的话，从她的倒影判断，她一定是一个衣裙整洁、楚楚动人、勤劳能干的小姑娘。她有一位年老体弱的妈妈，在暖和的日子里，老妈妈会在阳台上，坐在她身旁，小姑娘会为老妈妈披上披肩，拿枕头塞到她的椅背上作为靠垫，拿小凳子给她垫脚，偶尔小姑娘会放下手中的活计，亲吻轻抚母亲一小会儿，然后拾起活计重新工作，而这一切都让我兴致盎然。

　　时光荏苒，小姑娘渐渐长大，她的倒影也变长了，我猜，现在应该是一个十六七岁的大姑娘了吧？每天，我只能在一天中天光最亮的时候工作几个小时，所以我有大块时间来观察她的一举一动，并有足够的时间展开想象，在脑海中编织她的小小的传奇故事，赋予她以美丽，当然，很大程度上，这份美丽只是我想当然的结果。我看到了，或者说我幻想自己可以看到，她开始对我的倒影产生了兴趣（当然，她能看到我的倒影，就像我能看到她的倒影一样）。有一天，在我看来她正在直视着我的倒影，也就是说，她的倒影也正在看我，我使劲儿地向她点头致意，让我狂喜的是，她的倒影也在向我点头回应。这样，我们的倒影互相相识了。

　　每天早晨，老太太都会将我从床上挪到窗前的沙发上，等到傍晚少女离开阳台回去休息时再将我挪回床上，我很快就爱上了她，但是除了向她点头问候外，很长时间内我都打定主意仅限于此。然而有一天，当我注意到她的倒影在看我的倒影时，我便向她点头致意，接着向河里扔了一朵花,她几次向我点头作为回应,还让她的母亲看我扔的花。这样,每天早上我会向水中扔一朵花以示早安,傍晚再扔一朵花以示晚安。没过多久,我便发现我的心意都没有白费,因为有一天她也对着我的花扔了一朵。当看到两朵花缠在一起随波逐流时,她拊掌大笑。就这样,每天早晨和傍晚,我扔一朵花,她扔一朵花,当两朵花缠在一起时,她就会拍手,我也会拍手;但是当其中的一朵花受阻分开而不能一起同行时,她会举起双手假装很失望,而我也会尽力去模仿她的动作,尽管显得很英式,但模仿得很不像。而当花朵被过往的贡多拉小船突如其来地撞上之时(虽然这种情况不经常出现),她就会假装哭泣,我也会学她。这时,她会以手指天,就像一场好看的哑剧,表示这是天意让我们的花遭遇海难;我也会学她表演哑剧,虽然动作没她那么好看,告诉她下一次老天会慈悲些,或许明天我们的花朵会转运。这样一来二去,纯真的爱恋在继续。一天,她给我看她的十字架,还亲吻了十字架,我也亲吻一直在身边的一个小银质十字架,这样,她便已知晓,我们的信仰是一样的。

有一天,少女在阳台上没有出现,接下来的那几天也消失得无影无踪,虽然我还是照常扔花,但人和花却没有了伴侣。然而,一段时间过后,她又出现了,身着丧服,常常能听到她的哭声。我这才明白,原来这个可怜的孩子的母亲已经去世了,而据我所知,她在世界上再也没有亲人了。之后的很多天,她不再扔花朵,也不再表现出任何赞赏的迹象,眼睛只盯着手里的活计,只是用手绢擦拭眼泪。她的对面摆放着老夫人生前坐的那把椅子,我看得出,她会时不时地停下手头的活儿,凝视着椅子,泪流满面,让她有所释怀。最后,终于有一天,她起身向我点头,她的花儿也来了;日复一日,我也扔花参与,花朵也命运各异,随波逐流,一如从前。

但是，一个年轻英俊的贡多拉船夫笔直地站立在右侧船头（因为我能亲眼看到他），划着船沿屋过来，与坐在阳台上的她说话，这成了我生命中最黑暗的日子。看他们说话的样子像是老朋友，事实上，我能看出，他们说了足足半个小时，而他全程拉着她的手。最终，他摇船走了，却让我的心沉甸甸的。但是，我很快感恩起来，因为船夫走出视线以后，少女随即扔出长在一根茎上两朵花，开始我还没醒过味来，然后才恍然大悟，原来她想向我传达他们俩是兄妹的寓意，我不用为此伤心。于是，我高兴地向她点点头，她也对我点头，笑得很大声，我也大笑着回应，一切回转，一如从前。

接下来的日子是一段黑暗沉闷的日子，因为我必须接受治疗，所以缠绵病榻多日。我愁眉不展、烦躁不安起来，觉得我和那位少女再也不能相见，更糟的是，她会认为我是不辞而别。当夜晚来临，我失眠了，想怎样才能让她了解真相，我在心里制订出 50 个可行的计划，但是一早醒来，却觉得疯狂而不切实际。有一天，对我来说真是美好的一天啊，照料我的老太太告诉我，一位船夫在向她打听那位英国的先生是已经离开了还是去世了。我这才知道她一直都在担心我，所以派她哥哥来打听，而且毫无疑问，她的哥哥也已转告她我那么长时间没有在窗口出现的原因。

从那天起，以及随后我卧床不起的三个星期里，每天早上都会有一束花放在我的窗台上，窗台很低，任何人在船上都能轻而易举地够到。当我最终可以起床时，我坐在窗前的沙发上，一如从前。那位少女看见了我，她首尾颠倒着（从我的角度看），开心地拍着手，大喜过望，溢于言表，跟我一样。于是，那位船夫穿过我窗前时，我第一次向他挥手致意，于是他划到我的窗边，一脸灿烂的笑容，告诉我，看到我身体康复，他真的非常高兴。我向他以及他的妹妹表达谢意，谢谢他们在我患病期间那么多的美意。而且,我从他口中得知了她的名字叫作安吉拉,是全威尼斯最善良、最纯真的少女,能叫她妹妹的每个人确实都是幸福的,但是他却比做她的哥哥还要幸福。因为他即将娶她为妻,事实上,他们明天就要举行结婚典礼。

我的心跳加速,心简直快要蹦出来了,就在一瞬间,我什么也听不见,只听见血液在血管里奔流的声音。最终,我结结巴巴地送上了几句蹩脚的祝贺的话,而他,向我询问明天待他们从教堂归来后,是否可以带着他的新娘来看望我,随后,他哼着欢快的曲调离开了我。

他说:"我的安吉拉从小时候就认识你了,时间够长的。她经常向我谈起你这个虔诚天主教徒、可怜的英国人,长年累月地整日靠在窗前的沙发上。她反反复复地说,希望有朝一日可以和你说话,安慰你,当有一天你朝运河中扔一朵花以后,她问我她是否可以也扔一朵回应,我告诉她可以,因为你会明白,这是对痛苦不堪的人的同情。"

我这才明白,那不是爱情,是同情,只是类似于爱情的同情。这份同情使她愿意去关心我的幸福安康,一切都结束了。

我之前以为一根茎上的两朵花其实是两朵扎在一起的花(但我没有看出来),他们本意是想告诉我,他们是一对订婚了的爱人。而我对这束象征性的花所表达的喜悦却让她大喜过望,因为她以为这是我在为她的幸福而欢喜。

第二天,这位船夫以及众多的船友们,穿上节日的盛装,摇船而来;而安吉拉开心地坐在他的贡多拉小船上,幸福得双颊绯红。随后,他俩进了我的家,来到我的房间(感觉好奇怪啊,因为这些年都是看倒着的她,这是第一次看到她头在上脚在下地站着),她愿我幸福,身体快快好起来(那是不可能的)。我热泪盈眶,结结巴巴地祝福着,将放我床头柜上多年的银质小十字架送给了她,安吉拉虔诚地收下,画了十字，亲吻它，然后跟随喜气洋洋的新郎一道离开了。

　　船夫们伴着歌声上了路，慢慢消逝在远方，落日的余晖笼罩了我。我觉得他们唱的像是一首安魂曲，安慰那曾浸润我灵魂的唯一的爱情。

Angela, An Inverted Love Story

By William Schwenck Gilbert

I am a poor paralysed fellow who, for many years past, has been confined to a bed or a sofa. For the last six years I have occupied a small room, giving on to one of the side canals of Venice, and having no one about me but a deaf old woman, who makes my bed and attends to my food; and there I eke out a poor income of about thirty pounds a year by making water-colour drawings of flowers and fruit (they are the cheapest models in Venice), and these I send to a friend in London, who sells them to a dealer for small sums. But, on the whole, I am happy and content.

It is necessary that I should describe the position of my room rather minutely. Its only window is about five feet above the water of the canal, and above it the house projects some six feet, and overhangs the water, the projecting portion being supported by stout piles driven into the bed of the canal. This arrangement has the disadvantage (among others) of so limiting my upward view that I am unable to see more than about ten feet of the height of the house immediately opposite to me, although, by reaching as far out of the window as my infirmity will permit, I can see for a considerable distance up and down the canal, which does not exceed fifteen feet in width. But, although I can see but little of the material house opposite, I can see its reflection upside down in the canal, and I take a good deal of inverted interest in such of its inhabitants as show themselves from time to time (always upside down) on its balconies and at its windows.

When I first occupied my room, about six years ago, my attention was directed to the reflection of a little girl of thirteen or so (as nearly as I could judge), who passed every day on a balcony just above the upward range of my limited field of view. She had a glass of flowers and a crucifix on a little table by her side; and as she sat there, in fine weather, from early morning until dark, working assiduously all the time, I concluded that she earned her living by needle-work. She was certainly an industrious little girl, and, as far as I could judge by her upside-down reflection, neat in her dress and pretty. She had an old mother, an invalid, who, on warm days, would sit on the balcony with her, and it interested me to see the little maid wrap the old lady in shawls, and bring pillows for her chair, and a stool for her feet, and every now and again lay down her work and kiss and fondle the old lady for half a minute, and then take up her work again.

Time went by, and as the little maid grew up, her reflection grew down, and at last she was quite a little woman of, I suppose, sixteen or seventeen. I can only work for a couple of hours or so in the brightest part of the day, so I had plenty of time on my hands in which to watch her movements, and sufficient imagination to weave a little romance about her, and to endow her with a beauty which, to a great extent, I had to take for granted. I saw—or fancied that I could see—that she began to take an interest in my reflection (which, of course, she could see as I could see hers); and one day, when it appeared to me that she was looking right at it— that is to say when her reflection appeared to be looking right at me—I tried the desperate experiment of nodding to her, and to my intense delight her reflection nodded in reply. And so our two reflections became known to one another.

 It did not take me very long to fall in love with her, but a long time passed before I could make up my mind to do more than nod to her every morning, when the old woman moved me from my bed to the sofa at the window, and again in the evening, when the little maid left the balcony for that day. One day, however, when I saw her reflection looking at mine, I nodded to her, and threw a flower into the canal. She nodded several times in return, and I saw her direct her mother's attention to the incident. Then every morning I threw a flower into the water for 'good morning', and another in the evening for 'good night', and I soon discovered that I had not altogether thrown them in vain, for one day she threw a flower to join mine, and she laughed and clapped her hands when she saw the two flowers join forces and float away together. And then every morning and every evening she threw her flower when I threw mine, and when the two flowers met she clapped her hands, and so did I; but when they were separated, as they sometimes were, owing to one of them having met an obstruction which did not catch the other, she threw up her hands in a pretty affectation of despair, which I tried to imitate but in an English and unsuccessful fashion. And when they were rudely run down by a passing gondola (which happened not unfrequently) she pretended to cry, and I did the same. Then, in pretty pantomime, she would point downwards to the sky to tell me that it was Destiny that had caused the shipwreck of our flowers, and I, in pantomime, not nearly so pretty, would try to convey to her that Destiny would be kinder next time, and that perhaps tomorrow our flowers would be more fortunate—and so the innocent courtship went on. One day she showed me her crucifix and kissed it, and thereupon I took a little silver crucifix that always stood by me, and kissed that, and so she knew that we were one in religion.

One day the little maid did not appear on her balcony, and for several days I saw nothing of her; and although I threw my flowers as usual, no flower came to keep it company. However, after a time, she reappeared, dressed in black, and crying often, and then I knew that the poor child's mother was dead, and, as far as I knew, she was alone in the world. The flowers came no more for many days, nor did she show any sign of recognition, but kept her eyes on her work, except when she placed her handkerchief to them. And opposite to her was the old lady's chair, and I could see that, from time to time, she would lay down her work and gaze at it, and then a flood of tears would come to her relief. But at last one day she roused herself to nod to me, and then her flower came, day by day, and my flower went forth to join it, and with varying fortunes the two flowers sailed away as of yore.

But the darkest day of all to me was when a good-looking young gondolier, standing right end uppermost in his gondola (for I could see him in the flesh), worked his craft alongside the house, and stood talking to her as she sat on the balcony. They seemed to speak as old friends—indeed, as well as I could make out, he held her by the hand during the whole of their interview which lasted quite half an hour. Eventually he pushed off, and left my heart heavy within me. But I soon took heart of grace, for as soon as he was out of sight, the little maid threw two flowers growing on the same stem—an allegory of which I could make nothing, until it broke upon me that she meant to convey to me that he and she were brother and sister, and that I had no cause to be sad. And thereupon I nodded to her cheerily, and she nodded to me, and laughed aloud, and I laughed in return, and all went on again as before.

Then came a dark and dreary time, for it became necessary that I should undergo treatment that confined me absolutely to my bed for many days, and I worried and fretted to think that the little maid and I should see each other no longer, and worse still, that she would think that I had gone away without even hinting to her that I was going. And I lay awake at night wondering how I could let her know the truth, and fifty plans flitted through my brain, all appearing to be feasible enough at night, but absolutely wild and impracticable in the morning. One day—and it was a bright day indeed for me—the old woman who tended me told me that a gondolier had inquired whether the English signor had gone away or had died; and so I learnt that the little maid had been anxious about me, and that she had sent her brother to inquire, and the brother had no doubt taken to her the reason of my protracted absence from the window.

From that day, and ever after during my three weeks of bed-keeping, a flower was found every morning on the ledge of my window, which was within easy reach of anyone in a boat; and when at last a day came when I could be moved, I took my accustomed place on my sofa at the window, and the little maid saw me, and stood on her head (so to speak) and clapped her hands upside down with a delight that was as eloquent as my right-end-up delight could be. And so the first time the gondolier passed my window I beckoned to him, and he pushed alongside, and told me, with many bright smiles, that he was glad indeed to see me well again. Then I thanked him and his sister for their many kind thoughts about me during my retreat, and I then learnt from him that her name was Angela, and that she was the best and purest maiden in all Venice, and that anyone might think himself happy indeed who could call her sister, but that he was happier even than her brother, for he was to be married to her, and indeed they were to be married the next day.

Thereupon my heart seemed to swell to bursting, and the blood rushed through my veins so that I could hear it and nothing else for a while. I managed at last to stammer forth some words of awkward congratulation, and he left me, singing merrily, after asking permission to bring his bride to see me on the morrow as they returned from church.

"For," said he, "my Angela has known you very long—ever since she was a child, and she has often spoken to me of the poor Englishman who was a good Catholic, and who lay all day long for years and years on a sofa at a window, and she had said over and over again how dearly she wished she could speak to him and comfort him; and one day, when you threw a flower into the canal, she asked me whether she might throw another, and I told her yes, for he would understand that it meant sympathy for one sorely afflicted."

And so I learned that it was pity, and not love, except indeed such love as is akin to pity, that prompted her to interest herself in my welfare, and there was an end of it all.

For the two flowers that I thought were on one stem were two flowers tied together (but I could not tell that), and they were meant to indicate that she and the gondolier were affianced lovers, and my expressed pleasure at this symbol delighted her, for she took it to mean that I rejoiced in her happiness.

And the next day the gondolier came with a train of other gondoliers, all decked in their holiday garb, and on his gondola sat Angela, happy, and blushing at her happiness. Then he and she entered the house in which I dwelt, and came into my room (and it was strange indeed, after so many years of inversion, to see her with her head above her feet), and then she wished me happiness and a speedy restoration to good health (which could never be); and I in broken words and with tears in my eyes, gave her the little silver crucifix that had stood by my bed or my table for so many years. And Angela took it reverently, and crossed herself, and kissed it, and so departed with her delighted husband.

And as I heard the song of the gondoliers as they went their way—the song dying away in the distance as the shadows of the sundown closed around me—I felt that they were singing the requiem of the only love that had ever entered my heart.

一天的等待

[美国] 欧内斯特·海明威

当我们还躺在床上睡觉的时候,他走进屋里关上了窗户,我看到他好像是生病了的样子。他面色惨白,哆哆嗦嗦的,走路慢吞吞地,好像每走一步都痛似的。

"你怎么了,宝贝?"

"我头疼。"

"你最好还是回到床上去吧。"

"不用,我还好。"

"你回床上去吧。等我穿好衣服就来看你。"

可是,当我下楼来的时候,他已经穿好了衣服,正在火炉旁边坐着,看起来就是一个病势沉重、痛苦难当的九岁男孩。我把手放到他的额头上,发现他正在发高烧。

"你快上楼睡觉去吧。"我说。"你生病了。"

"我还好。"他说。

这时医生进来给儿子测量了体温。

"怎么样,多少度?"我问他。

"102度。"

在楼下，医生留下了三种药，三种不同颜色的胶囊，并且告诉他服药方法。一种是退烧药，另一种是通便药，第三种是控制酸性状态的药。医生还解释说，流感病菌只会在酸性状态中存活。他似乎对流感无所不知，还说只要体温不高于104度就不用担心。这是轻度流感，只要不得肺炎，就没有什么危险。

回到房间以后我把男孩的体温记了下来，还一一记录了服用不同药物的时间。

"你想让我读书给你听吗？"

"好吧，你想念就念吧。"男孩说。他面色惨白，眼睛下面还有黑眼圈。他躺在床上纹丝不动，好像很疏离，对外界一点都不感兴趣。

我大声念着霍华德·派尔的《海盗故事》，但我能看得出来他根本没听我念的是什么内容。

"现在感觉怎么样，宝贝？"我问他。

"到目前为止，还是老样子。"他说。

我坐在床尾一边自己看书，一边等着到了时间给他吃另一种药。本来他睡觉是自然而然的事情，但我抬眼一看他正盯着床尾，那样子非常奇怪。

"你怎么不眯一会儿呢？到了吃药的时候我会叫你的。"

"我宁愿醒着。"

不一会儿，他对我说："爸爸，要是打扰你，你就不用在这陪我了。"

"没打扰我。"

"不，我的意思是说，如果这里叫你心烦的话，就不用非得待在这陪我了。"

我想或许他有点神志不清，到了十一点我给他吃了医生开的胶囊后就到外面待了一会儿。

那天万里无云,但气温很低,地上覆盖着一层雨夹雪后冻成的冰,因此,所有光秃秃的树木、灌木丛、修剪过的灌木,所有草地和空地上面好像都涂上了一层冰似的。我带着一条爱尔兰长毛小猎犬沿着那条路,沿着一条结冰的小河散步,但是在光滑的路面上站立或是行走都很困难,这条红毛小狗溜了一下就滑倒了,我也摔了两跤,摔得还挺重,我的枪都脱手了一次,在冰上滑走了。

我们惊起了一群在土堤下高高的灌木丛中躲藏的鹌鹑,它们从土堤顶上飞走时我打死了两只。有些鹌鹑转移到了树上,但大多数都四散在一丛丛灌木林间,你必须在长着灌木丛的结冰的土墩上蹦跳几下,它们才会惊起。你还在覆盖着冰雪的、富有弹性的灌木丛里摇摇晃晃,竭力保持身体平衡的时候,它们这才飞出来,这时要击中它们绝非易事,我射中了两只,没射中五只,动身回来时,发现靠近家舍附近也有一群鹌鹑,心内欢喜,因为第二天还可以找到这么多鹌鹑。

到家后,家人说,儿子拒绝让任何人进他房间。

"你们不能进来,"他说,"你们绝不能拿走我的东西。"

我上楼去看他,发现他纹丝没动,还保持着我离开他时候的那个姿势,脸色惨白,不过因为发烧,脸颊红红的,还是像刚才那样一动不动死死地盯着床尾。

我给他量了体温。

"多少度?"

"好像是100度,"我说。实际是102.4度。

"是102度。"他说。

"谁说的?"

"医生说的。"

"你的体温还好,"我说,"没什么好担心的。"

"我不担心,"他说,"但是我不得不想。"

"别想了,"我说,"放松点。"

"我在放松。"他说着,眼睛直勾勾地朝前看。很明显他在掩藏着什么心事。

"喝水吃药吧。"

"你觉得这药吃了能顶用吗?"

"当然有用啦。"

我坐下来,又翻开了《海盗故事》,开始念给他听。但看得出他听不进去,于是,我就不念了。

"你认为我会什么时候死呢?"他问道。

"你说什么?"

"我还能活多长时间?"

"你不会死的。你怎么啦?"

"哦,我会死的。我听见他说102度了。"

"人发烧到102度是不会死的。真是在说傻话呢。"

"我知道会死的。在法国上学的时候,我就听同学说,人烧到44度就不能活了。我已经到102度了。"

原来从早上九点钟起,他就一直在等死,都等了一整天了。

"你这个可怜的宝贝,"我说,"可怜的大宝贝啊,这就好比英里和公里。你不会死的。那是两种不同的体温表。那种表上37度算正常。这种表要98度才算正常。"

"你肯定?"

"绝对肯定!"我说。"这就好比英里和公里。你知道我们开车时车速70英里等于多少公里吗?"

"哦。"他说。

可他盯住床尾的眼光慢慢和缓了下来,他内心的紧张焦虑最后也终于轻松了,第二天一点也不紧张了,他还为了一点鸡毛蒜皮的小事哭鼻子呢。

世界有时残酷　但爱从未缺席

A Day's Wait

By Ernest Hemingway

He came into the room to shut the windows while we were still in bed and I saw he looked ill. He was shivering, his face was white, and he walked slowly as though it ached to move.

"What's the matter, Schatz?"

"I've got a headache."

"You better go back to bed."

"No. I'm all right."

"You go to bed. I'll see you when I'm dressed."

But when I came downstairs he was dressed, sitting by the fire, looking a very sick and miserable boy of nine years. When I put my hand on his forehead I knew he had a fever.

"You go up to bed," I said, "you're sick."

"I'm all right." he said.

When the doctor came he took the boy's temperature.

"What is it?" I asked him.

"One hundred and two."

Downstairs, the doctor left three different medicines in different colored capsules with instructions for giving them. One was to bring down the fever, another a purgative, the third to overcome an acid condition. The germs of influenza can only exist in an acid condition, he explained. He seemed to know all about influenza and said there was nothing to worry about if the fever did not go above one hundred and four degrees. This was a light epidemic of flu and there was no danger if you avoided pneumonia.

Back in the room I wrote the boy's temperature down and made a note of the time to give the various capsules.

"Do you want me to read to you?"

"All right. If you want to." said the boy. His face was very white and there were dark areas under his eyes. He lay still in the bed and seemed very detached from what was going on.

I read aloud from Howard Pyle's Book of Pirates; but I could see he was not following what I was reading.

"How do you feel, Schatz?" I asked him.

"Just the same, so far." he said.

I sat at the foot of the bed and read to myself while I waited for it to be time to give another capsule. It would have been natural for him to go to sleep, but when I looked up he was looking at the foot of the bed, looking very strangely.

"Why don't you try to go to sleep? I'll wake you up for the

medicine."

"I'd rather stay awake."

After a while he said to me, "You don't have to stay in here with me, Papa, if it bothers you."

"It doesn't bother me."

"No, I mean you don't have to stay if it's going to bother you."

I thought perhaps he was a little lightheaded and after giving him the prescribed capsules at eleven o'clock I went out for a while.

It was a bright, cold day, the ground covered with a sleet that had frozen so that it seemed as if all the bare trees, the bushes, the cut brush and all the grass and the bare ground had been varnished with ice. I took the young Irish setter for a little walk up the road and along a frozen creek, but it was difficult to stand or walk on the glassy surface and the red dog slipped and slithered and I fell twice, hard, once dropping my gun and having it slide away over the ice.

We flushed a covey of quail under a high clay bank with overhanging brush and I killed two as they went out of sight over the top of the bank. Some of the covey lit in trees, but most of them scattered into brush piles and it was necessary to jump on the ice-coated mounds of brush several times before they would flush. Coming out while you were poised unsteadily on the icy, springy brush they made difficult shooting and I killed two, missed five, and started back pleased to have found a covey close to the house and happy there were so many left to find on another day.

At the house they said the boy had refused to let any one come into the room.

"You can't come in." he said, "You mustn't get what I have."

I went up to him and found him in exactly the position I had left him, white-faced, but with the tops of his cheeks flushed by the fever, staring still, as he had stared, at the foot of the bed.

I took his temperature.

"What is it?"

"Something like a hundred." I said. It was one hundred and two and four tenths.

"It was a hundred and two." he said.

"Who said so?"

"The doctor."

"Your temperature is all right." I said, "It's nothing to worry about."

"I don't worry," he said, "but I can't keep from thinking."

"Don't think." I said, "Just take it easy."

"I'm taking it easy," he said and looked straight-ahead. He was evidently holding tight onto himself about something.

"Take this with water."

"Do you think it will do any good?"

"Of course will."

I sat down and opened the Pirate book and commenced to read but I could see he was not following, so I stopped.

"About what time do you think I'm going to die?" he asked.

"What?"

"About how long will it be before I die?"

"You aren't going to die. What's the matter with you?"

"Oh, yes, I am. I heard him say a hundred and two."

"People don't die with a fever of one hundred and two. That's a silly way to talk."

"I know they do. At school in France, the boys told me you can't live with forty-four degrees. I've got a hundred and two."

He had been waiting to die all day, ever since nine o'clock in the morning.

"You poor Schatz." I said, "Poor old Schatz. It's like miles and kilometres. You aren't going to die. That's a different thermometer. On that thermometer thirty-seven is normal. On this kind it's ninety-eight."

"Are you sure?"

"Absolutely." I said, "It's like miles and kilometers. You know, like how many kilometers we make when we do seventy miles in the car?"

"Oh." he said.

But his gaze at the foot of the bed relaxed slowly. The hold over himself relaxed too, finally, and the next day it was very slack and he cried very easily at little things that were of no importance.

机器人保姆

[英国] 乔恩·朗格弗德

我一开始就心存疑虑,不过话又说回来,我对新技术素来都是心存疑虑的。

事情是这样的,我所有的朋友都买了伯蒂牌(BERTIE)机器人,因此,我太太几个月来一直缠着我也去买一台。实话实说,只要能让她闭上嘴,就值得买。

伯蒂是一个机器人,像做饭、打扫卫生、洗衣服这些家务事,他都可以高效地完成,这下你明白了吧?(我们所购买的)伯蒂二代机器人甚至可以遛狗,辅导孩子做作业,还会给我妻子按摩(这也是她最喜欢的)。

BERTIE 是"为智能进化而训练的仿生机器人"的英文缩写。这就意味着伯蒂将会学习到一个家庭所具有的 PID(个性、特质和动态性),而且不断地做出相应调整以更好适应其所处的环境。想买伯蒂的家人们当然喜欢这几个缩略词了,我也就成全他们。

现在,我承认,在这个小玩意儿(也可以认为他是个奴隶?)身上花费两万美元确实有点多,可我们发现,长远来看我们不只会省下钱,更重要的是,还会省下时间。于是,我们解雇了保姆和清洁工,在一个平平常常的周四,我带着一台伯蒂回家了。

在使用伯蒂前,首先你必须给他充电24个小时。那个站在角落里像人一般的机器人,正不断地从电源里汲取着他生命所需的能量,我和妻子、女儿,还有狗,一起坐在客厅里目不转睛地看着,着了迷。

"他看起来像是真人,"我的女儿说,"简直和我们一模一样。"

"上面说他的头发就是真人的头发。"我的妻子读着伯蒂包装箱背面的文字,说道。

我看了看这个机器人的头发,这该死的家伙的头发竟然比我的头发还要浓密,让我很恼火。接着我便开始想他的头发是从哪里来的,是从死人头上剪下来的吗?还是制造商花钱从活人手里买来的呢?可无论是什么来路,都让人恶心。我不知道他们为什么要把他造得活灵活现,这么像人类。看在上帝的分儿上,他只是个机器人罢了,那看起来就应该像个机器人,而不应该像一个44岁老男人,皮肤完美像牛奶般光滑,这让人感到毛骨悚然。

这时,克洛伊从沙发上站起来,走到伯蒂正在充电的地方。

"不要靠得太近。"我提醒着她,就像一位父亲看着孩子走近悬崖边,是父母惯有的警告的口吻。

她举起一只小手,轻轻地摸着机器人的脸。就在那时,伯蒂毫无预兆地突然活了,他的脑袋晃了晃,眼珠也动了起来。克洛伊顿时尖声大叫,跑了出去,洛根则从咖啡桌上跳了过去,不信任地冲他狂吠起来。

"您好,我的名字叫伯蒂,我来这里是为了让您的生活更轻松。"他说道。

有了伯蒂还不到一个月的时间,我们五个——我、我妻子、克洛伊、洛根和伯蒂挤进一辆车,去公园玩一天,带着伯蒂是为了让他准备野餐，清理我们留下的垃圾。好了，另一个家庭紧挨着我们坐了下来，正当他们拿出食物之际，洛根跑过去，开始打扰他们。我大声喊了他好多次，可他就是不肯回来。我起身准备过去把他抓回来，可就在那时，伯蒂突然叫了他一声，他马上就回来了。我明白，他在这个机器人面前言听计从。

我的机器人偷走了我的狗，偷走本应该属于我的那份忠诚。那天剩下的时间里我都气呼呼的，百思不得其解。我太太一直在追问我，"你怎么不说话了，是哪里不舒服吗？"这就更是火上浇油了，我讨厌她那么问我。

过了好多天，就在我去上班的路上，我忽然意识到我答应借给同事的球推杆忘了带，我便立即掉转车头回家。

刚一到家，死一般的沉寂扑面袭来，接着我便向后屋走去。一阵低低的呻吟声从客房传来，我停下了脚步侧耳倾听，那是我太太的声音。接着，她又呻吟起来，声音更大了，声音在空中萦绕了片刻。这声音简直和我们做爱时她发出的声音一模一样。

我向客房门前挪近了几步，带着一种怀疑，甚至有些期待的心境偷偷靠近。倘若她有私情，那她就给我提供了一条出路。

接着，她发出了一声快乐的尖叫，"哦，这感觉真是太太太太棒了！"

我一把将门推开，只见我太太人趴着，未着上衣，脊椎底部盖着一条毛巾。机器人站在她身旁，双手搭在她的肩上。

"这是怎么回事？"我觉得有点好笑，又有点茫然地问道。

我太太看起来羞愧难当。可机器人还在继续给她按摩，机器人就是这样，你没让他停，他就根本停不下来。

"哦，嗨，"我太太回答道，"你回家来做什么？我只是在做做按摩。"

"是的,"我说,"我看得出来,而且听得出来你还挺享受呢!"

"哦,别说啦!你回家到底是为什么,说实话!"

那天剩下的时间里,我总是忍不住回想起我太太看到我站在门口时脸上流露出的神情,她看起来羞愧难当,我还不如捉奸在床呢!我还总是忍不住地回想起在我出现前,她发出的那充满快乐的呻吟之声,看得出,她从机器人的触摸中得到的快感比我多年来给她的多。

又过了几星期,那天是周末,我在家准备晚饭,我太太拿定主意想吃我们曾在马德里一家餐馆曾经吃过的饭菜,当时那顿饭我们吃的几乎算得上是愉快。

伯蒂(在他的大脑里)下载了食谱,出去买了食材,准备烹制。五小时后,他喊我们到餐桌吃饭。我不得不承认,饭菜做得简直太美味了!机器人祝我们用餐愉快,然后离开了。

"我想我们应该让伯蒂和我们一起用餐。"我太太说道。

"好耶!"克洛伊说。

"什么?"我说。

妻子说:"这是理所当然的,这顿饭他做得这么辛苦,看在上帝的分儿上,他在厨房里从中午一直工作到现在,让我们邀请他与我们共进晚餐吧,我不想让他有冷落之感。"

我答道:"你说的话错误太多,我都不知道该从哪里说起。第一,伯蒂是个机器人,他不能吃饭,他之所以能站在这里是因为充了电;第二,他是个机器,不具备感知情绪的能力,所以他根本不会有冷落之感。就像说:'哦,电视机一定很累,它整天都在工作,我们今晚为什么不与它同床共眠呢?'"

"我就是想要伯蒂嘛!"克洛伊哭喊着说。

晚餐结束后，妻子叫来了伯蒂，我坐在那里，默默无语，他们三个竟在饭桌上玩起了文字游戏，我在自己的家里反倒像个不速之客。

几个月过去了，我太太总是和我说伯蒂是多么令人惊叹，她是怎么才有那么多的空闲时间去做更多的事，我听了开怀大笑起来。她那双手除了戴昂贵的珠宝外，唯一拥有的就是时间了。她没有工作，也从没工作过，她所做的也只有购物，和朋友约会共进午餐。甚至就在伯蒂来的前几天，我们还雇着保姆和清洁工。无论如何，她总是一直在和我说伯蒂和克洛伊相处得多么多么融洽，他们在晚饭后是怎样一起玩棋盘游戏，还有她"简直无法想象，没有伯蒂的生活要怎么过"（这是她的原话）。

一天夜里，我设法早早摆脱工作，想在克洛伊睡觉前回到家。等我来到客厅，他们三个竟围坐在咖啡桌旁，玩着垄断大亨的游戏。我等他们玩完了游戏，嘱咐克洛伊去刷牙，准备睡觉。我告诉伯蒂给我来杯加奎宁水的杜松子酒，然后去给克洛伊掖被子，给她讲着故事。故事说完，我吻了吻她的额头，给她关了床头灯，把门留了一个小缝儿，好让楼梯口的灯光照进来，她喜欢这样。

"可是爸爸，"她说，"伯蒂还没有对我说晚安呢！"

"什么？"

"伯蒂也得给我讲故事才行，他一直都是这样的。"

"我想他在忙吧。"我回答道。

"求你了，爸爸，求求你了！"

"不行，伯蒂很忙，现在就睡觉！"

她开始放声大哭了起来，我把伯蒂带来，她才住了声。

后来，深夜了，我让伯蒂出去遛狗，这样我才有了和太太私聊的机会。

"这种情况持续多久了？"我一边喝着加奎宁水的杜松子酒，一边问道，不得不承认，伯蒂调制的加奎宁水的杜松子酒很好喝。

"这不能怪我，你总是工作到那么晚。"她总是以一种消极抵触的语调和我说话，任何时候都是如此。

"哦，又来了。"我说，"一如既往，这都是我的错。你知道，必须有人要去赚钱，我们才有舒适豪华的公寓住，才能买得起精致美丽的东西，就像你新买的自拍神器。"

"可是，对她来说，那个机器人比你更像她的父亲。"妻子说。

你可以想象一下，我的心是多么痛啊！那晚，我没有和她同床共眠，而是睡在了客房。在凌晨的某个时段，我因喉咙干涩而醒来，需要喝水，于是我拿起空空的杯子，向厨房走去。可还没走到厨房，我就看到那里亮着灯。这很是奇怪，因为我太太对关灯这件事十分挑剔。通过门框间狭窄的缝隙，我看到机器人坐在餐桌旁，看着一本书。

当我走进厨房，发现那并不是一本书，而是一本家庭相册，我家的家庭相册。

"你在做什么？"我说。

"请原谅，先生，"他说，"我只是想看看这些相册，想一想记忆是什么感觉？我的意思是，我有记忆，可我没有情感'记忆'，我就想知道……拥有情感'记忆'会是什么感觉？"

"有趣的问题，"我说，"记忆就像是……"就在那时，我按下了这个家伙的开关，他脖子后面有一个开关。

BERTIE

By Jon Langford

I was skeptical at first, but then again, I always am where new technology's concerned.

The thing is, all my friends had a BERTIE and my wife had been pestering me to buy one for months. And to be totally honest with you, it was worth buying one just to get her to shut the hell up.

BERTIE is a robot that efficiently performs domestic tasks like cooking, cleaning, laundry...you get the picture. The second generation BERTIE (the one that we got) can even walk the dog, help the kids with their homework and (my wife's favorite) give massages.

BERTIE stands for Bionically Engineered Robot Trained for Intelligent Evolution. What this means is that BERTIE will learn the family's PID (personality, idiosyncrasies, dynamic) and adjust itself accordingly to better suit its environment. The folks over at BERTIE HQ certainly love their acronyms; I'll give them that.

Now, I'll admit twenty thousand dollars is a lot to spend on a gadget (or is it a slave?) but we figured we'd save money in the long term and, more importantly, we'd save time. So we fired the nanny and the cleaner and on no particular Tuesday I came home with a BERTIE.

Before you can use BERTIE you must first charge it for twenty-four hours. My wife, daughter, the dog and I, sat in the living room and watched, fascinated, as the humanoid in the corner stood sapping the electricity it needed for life from the mains.

"It looks so real," said my daughter, Chloe. "Just like us."

"It says here his hair is real human hair," said my wife, reading from the back of BERTIE's box.

I looked at the robot's hair. It pissed me off. That son of a bitch had a thicker mane than me. Then I started thinking about where the hair came from. Was it from a dead human? Or did the manufacturer pay people for their hair? Either option was gross. I don't know why they make it so human looking. It's a robot for God's sake; it should look like a robot, not a creepy forty-four year-old man with flawless milky skin.

Chloe got up off the couch and walked over to where BERTIE was charging.

"Don't get too close to it," I said with the parental caution of a father watching his child approach the ledge of a cliff.

She lifted her small hand and touched the robot's face. Then, without warning, it suddenly came to life. Its head jolted up and the eyes came alive. Chloe screamed and ran away. Logan leapt over the coffee table and barked at it with mistrust.

"Hello, my name is Bertie," it said, "and I'm here to make your life easier."

Less than a month after getting BERTIE the five of us (me, the wife, Chloe, Logan and BERTIE) piled into the car and went for a day at the park. We took BERTIE to prepare the picnic and clean up after us. Anyway, there was another family sitting close by and when they got their food out Logan ran over and started bothering them. I called him, several times, but he would not come. I got up to go and grab him when all of a sudden BERTIE called him and he came right away, and, get this, he heeled in front of the robot.

My robot had stolen my dog's loyalty. I was quiet the rest of the day. Pissed off and confused. My wife kept asking me, "Are you okay? You're being quiet. What's wrong?" and that pissed me off even more. I hate when she asks me that.

Days later, on my way to work, I realized I'd forgotten the putter I'd promised to lend a work colleague. I spun the car round and headed back home.

It was dead silent when I let myself in. Then, as I headed toward the back room, I heard a low groan coming from the guestroom. I stopped and listened. It was my wife. Then she moaned again, louder, letting it hang in the air for a moment, the same way she did when we used to have sex.

I took a few steps closer to the guestroom door, stalking, suspicious, hopeful even. If she was having an affair, it would offer me a way out.

Then she let out a squeal of delight: "Oh that feels so good!"

I pushed the door open and saw my wife lying naked on her belly, a towel pulled up to the bottom of her spine. The robot was standing over her, his hands on her shoulders.

"What's going on here?" I said, slightly amused, slightly bemused.

My wife looked guilty as hell. The robot kept on massaging. They keep on doing things until you tell them to stop.

"Oh hi," said my wife. "What are you doing home? I'm just having a massage."

"Yeah," I said. "I can see that. It sounded like you were enjoying it too."

"Oh shut up!" she said. "What are you doing home, seriously?"

For the rest of the day I couldn't stop thinking about the look on my wife's face when she saw me in the doorway. She looked so guilty. I may as well have caught her screwing around. I also couldn't stop thinking about the pleasure-filled moans she was letting out until I came along. She was getting more pleasure from the robot's touch than I'd given her in years.

A few weeks later, it was on the weekend because I was home for dinner, my wife decided that she wanted to eat food from the menu of a restaurant we once ate at in Madrid, back when we were something close to happy.

BERTIE downloaded the recipe (in his head), went out for ingredients and got to work. Five hours later he called us to the dinner table. It looked fantastic, I have to admit. The robot wished us bon appetit and left.

"I think we should ask Bertie to eat with us," said my wife.

"Yay!" said Chloe.

"What?" I said.

"It's only right," said my wife. "He worked so hard on this meal. He's been in the kitchen since noon for God's sake. Let's ask him to eat with us; I don't want him to feel left out."

"There's so many things wrong with what you're saying that I don't know where to start," I said. "Bertie is a robot. He doesn't eat food; he eats electricity so he would just be sitting there. Second, he doesn't feel left out, he's a machine and incapable of that emotion. That's like saying: 'Oh, the television must be tired because it's been on all day, why don't we let it sleep in bed with us tonight?'"

"I want Bertie!" cried Chloe.

My wife called BERTIE in and I sat there in silence while the three of them played word games over dinner. I felt like an unwelcome guest in my own home.

A few more months passed and my wife kept telling me how amazing BERTIE was. How she had so much more time on her hands to do things. That made me laugh. The only thing she's ever had on her hands besides expensive jewelry is time. She doesn't work, never has. All she does is shop and have lunch dates with friends. Even in the pre-BERTIE days we had a nanny and a cleaner. Anyway, she kept telling me how great BERTIE was with Chloe, how they all played board games together after dinner and how she "couldn't imagine life without him" (actual quote).

One night I'd managed to get out of work early and made it home before Chloe's bedtime. I came into the living room and the three of them were sat around the coffee table playing Monopoly. I let them finish the game and then sent Chloe off to brush her teeth and get ready for bed. I told BERTIE to fix me a gin and tonic and then I went to tuck Chloe in and read her a story. When I was done I kissed her forehead, turned out her lamp and pulled the door to, leaving a gap an inch thick to allow light from the landing to bleed in, just the way she likes it.

"But Daddy," she said. "Bertie hasn't said goodnight to me yet."

"What?"

"Bertie has to read me a story too. He always does."

"I think he's busy," I said.

"Please Daddy, please."

"No. Bertie's busy. Now go to sleep."

She started crying and wouldn't stop until I sent BERTIE in.

Later that night, I sent BERTIE out to walk the dog so I could talk to my wife in private.

"How long has this been going on?" I asked sipping on my gin and tonic, which I have to admit, was very well made.

"It's not my fault that you're always working late," she said in the passive-aggressive tone she used whenever she said anything to me.

"Oh here we go again," I said. "It's all my fault as usual. You know, someone has to earn money so we can live in a nice apartment and buy nice things like your new iMirror."

"That robot's been more of a father to her than you ever have," said my wife.

You can imagine how much that one hurt. I couldn't share a bed with her that night so I decided to sleep in the guestroom. Sometime during the small hours I woke with a dry throat and needed water. I picked up my empty glass and went through to the kitchen. Before I got there I could see that the kitchen light was on. It was strange because one thing about my wife, she's anal about turning off lights. Through the narrow gap between the door and frame I could see the robot. It was sitting at the kitchen table, looking at a book.

When I got in the kitchen I saw that it wasn't a book. It was a family photo album. My family photo album.

"What are you doing?" I said.

"Forgive me, Sir," it said. "I was just looking at photo albums and I got to thinking, what do memories feel like? I mean, I have memory but I don't have memories, in the emotional sense, and I was wondering…what do they feel like?"

"Interesting question," I said. "Memories are like…" Then I shut the bastard off. There's a switch on the back of his neck.

译后记

常常有初涉翻译的同学问我，做好翻译需要哪些过程？其实，这跟做其他学术研究也没有什么不同，无非还是那"三板斧"——理论、历史、实践。具体到翻译上，就是翻译理论，包括具有描述、解释、预测功能的纯翻译理论，以及指导功能的应用翻译理论，具有借鉴功能的翻译史，还具有实用功能的翻译实践。

法国哲学家帕斯卡说过："智慧胜于知识。"如果说，知识回答的"是什么"，那么，智慧回答的就是"怎么样"和"为什么"。对于翻译来说，翻译理论和翻译史解决的是宏观层面"何为译"的问题；文化，特别是语言对比解决的是"译何为"的问题；从语法、逻辑、修辞三个维度审视翻译实践解决"如何译"的问题。当然，翻译是一个需要 know something about everything 的专业，也就是 "you don't need to know everything about something, but you need to know a little bit of everything"，掌握一些翻译辅助工具也很有必要。

对于翻译理论，我曾在专著《翻译基础指津》（中译出版社，2017年）中有过专题阐述，这里就不再赘述，说到底，科学的核心是理论，没有理论，你的研究将一无所有。

对于翻译理论与实践之间的关系，要明确的是离开实践的理论是空洞的理论，离开理论的实践是盲目的实践。

翻译是一种看似门槛很低、实则难度很高的学术。其实，不是学语言的都是学英语的；不是学英语的都能做翻译；不是做翻译的什么文体都能翻译。相对于母语创作来说，翻译创作的难度更高。对于英语专业来说，听说读写译，最难莫过于翻译；对于各种翻译文体来说，最难莫过于文学翻译。至于翻译标准，我觉得上下文，也只有上下文，才是决定词义、段义、句义、文义的唯一标准。这个上下文可以是上一个词和下一个词，也可以是上一句和下一句，或者是上一段和下一段，甚至是上一章和下一章，乃至同一作者所著的上一部作品和下一部作品。具体践行到中观层面，双语差异之处，便是困难之时。到了微观层面，译得通不通是语法问题，译得对不对是逻辑问题，译得好不好是修辞问题。

下面，就以之前翻译的图书为例，来做一简要的实证。

一、逻辑

例1. Do you understand what condoms are used for?

你知道安全套是用来做什么的吗？

——《谋杀的颜色》

（原文中被问的是一个14岁的孩子，所以condom虽然是一个专有名词，通常选择一个义项即可，但考虑到孩子对性的有限认知,这里只能译成"安全套",不能译成"避孕套"。)

例2. She had been older than he then in Ohio. Now she was not young at all. Bill was still young.

当年在俄亥俄州的时候她就比他大,现在,她毕竟已经不再年轻,而比尔却不见老。

——译趣坊第一辑《时光不会辜负有爱的人》之《初秋》

(原文 Bill was still young 是肯定形式,译文转换成了否定形式,但内容没有变,反而更为准确。)

例3. God made Coke, God made Pepsi, God made me, oh so sexy, God made rivers, God made lakes, God made you…well we all make mistakes.

上帝创造了可口可乐,上帝创造了百事可乐,上帝创造了我,哦,多么性感。上帝创造了河流,上帝创造了湖泊,上帝创造了你……怎么说呢,谁能不出错呢?

——译趣坊第一辑《人生是一场意外的遇见》之《毒舌段子》

(原文的 well we all make mistakes 译成了"怎么说呢,谁能不出错呢?"肯定变否定,句号变问号,但内在的逻辑始终如一。)

二、语法

例1. "Do you think all these people are happy with the wonderful things they have?" She asked.

"People happy with things? No, no," the old man said. "Only people make people happy. You just have to know how to love people. People aren't things; people think, they feel. You have to tell them you love them. You have to show them. You have to say nice things. You have to mean them…"

"你觉得这些拥有好东西的人幸福吗？"她问道。

"拥有东西的人幸福？不对，不对，"老人说道，"只有人才能让人幸福。你需要知道怎么去爱别人就够了。人不是东西；人会思考，人有感觉。你要告诉别人你爱他们，你要把爱展示给他们看。你要说金玉良言，要有真情实感……"

——译趣坊第一辑《愿你出走半生　归来仍是少年》之《幸福在哪里》

（关于一词多义，就是要"确认过眼神，选择对的含义"。原文的 wonderful things 在上下文中有哲学意味，指代的是物质，这里在讨论的实际上是物质和精神与幸福之间的关系，所以译成"东西"；You have to say nice things 里的 things 指的是话语，所以译成了"金玉良言"。）

例 2. Saying goodbye in autumn is not saying goodbye forever.

对秋天说再见，秋天还会见。

——《英汉经典阅读系列散文卷》之《乡村之秋》

（关于句法翻译，要分析原文的句子成分，先找出主谓宾，然后找出定状补,确定句意。双语能"神同步"真真是极好的。不能就或分或合,或缩或扩,或换序,或变性、变态,甚至十八般武艺并用,舍"形"而取"义"。从语言层次的转换情况来看,既可以是同一层次的同类型转换,也可以是同一层次的非同类型转换,还可以是超越同一层次的转换。从本句来看,译文做了分句处理,属于同一类型的非同类型转换。)

例3. I loved you enough to accept you for what you are, not what I wanted you to be.

我爱你至深,才接受你现在的样子,尽管不是我期望的样子。

——译趣坊第一辑《时光不会辜负有爱的人》之《爱你至深》

(关于从句翻译,原文的 what you are 和 what I wanted you to be 实现了从句译成词组,句型由抽象向具体的转换。)

例4. They are hard to find when your eyes are closed, but they are everywhere you look when you choose to see.

选择合上双眼,天使很难发现;选择睁大双眼,天使会在任何地方出现。

——译趣坊第二辑《生命中一直在等待的那一天》之《天使何所似》

(英文重形合,句子成分"一个都不能少",所以连词、关系词、介词多,译成汉语,很多时候,一省了之。原文的 when 和 but 就是如此。)

例 5. "You're a very good dancer," she sighed.

"你的舞跳得好好啊！"她叹道。

——译趣坊第三辑《愿我们每个人都被世界温柔以待》之《下雨天，留人天》

（在翻译过程中，英汉两种语言的词类或词性均会经常发生转换。没有什么词是不能"变性"的，本句原文的名词 dancer 就译成了动词"跳"。从本质上讲，汉语是一种多运用动词的语言，是真正的"动感地带"。）

三、修辞

例 1. Alarmed, sad? He smiled, and his smile kept on getting broader, and before long, he was dissolving into laughter. He was determined to control himself, but this resistance collapsed completely. He started guffawing loudly…

感到奇怪？难过？他微微笑着，接着，嘴越咧越大，迸发出一声大笑，他想自控，但这一抵抗立刻土崩瓦解了，竟哈哈大笑不止。

——译趣坊第一辑《愿你出走半生　归来仍是少年》之《幸福的人》

（这是层递修辞格，程度递增，直译过来，一目了然。）

例 2. May you always walk your path with love. May you always help your fellow travelers along the way. And may your roads always lead you Home again.

愿你的人生之路都有爱为伴,愿你在旅途中帮助同路人,愿你人生中的一段又一段旅程都是通往回"家"的路。

——译趣坊第二辑《所有的路 最终都是回家的路》之《所有的路,最终都是回家的路》

(这是重复修辞格,译文三个"愿你",一一对应,句句对应,原文 roads 的复数得到强化翻译,作为全篇收尾的画龙点睛之笔。)

例3. Even more than what they eat I like their intellectual grasp. It is wonderful. Just watch them read. They simply read all the time.

我喜欢他们的饮食,但是我更喜欢他们学富五车。那真是了不起。看看他们看的书就一目了然了。他们简直就是手不释卷。

——译趣坊第三辑《如果事与愿违 请相信一定另有安排》之《怎样成为百万富翁》

(修辞翻译也可以"无中生有",本句中的 intellectual grasp 译成"学富五车"、read all the time 译成"手不释卷",也都毫无违和感。)

例4. Neither manifested the least disposition to retreat. It was evident that their battle-cry was "Conquer or die".

双方都没有一丝一毫的退却表现,显然他们的战争口号是"不成功便成仁"。

——译趣坊第三辑《选一种姿态 让自己活得无可替代》之

《红蚂蚁大战黑蚂蚁》

（修辞可以让你的译文变得更有腔调。"想要有腔调，就不能说大白话，得加上装饰"。原文中的 Conquer or die 是一个仿拟修辞格，以归化的策略套译成"不成功便成仁"，来描绘双方死战的状态，成为亲切的"中国风"。）

Language is shaped by, and shapes, human thought. 这句话的意思是"人的思想形成语言，而语言又影响了人的思想。"文学翻译是一个在各美其美、美人之美的基础上，力争美美与共的过程。原作者的思想形成了原作者的语言，原作者的语言又影响了我的思想。文学翻译让我意识到：文学的终极使命，是一种灵魂的救赎，我庆幸自己此生在一个不合时宜的时空做了一件不合时宜的事情，它唤醒了我心中一个蠢蠢欲动的自己。我爱这个自己，我相信文学"他者"的魔力，可以让一只匍匐的虫豸，陡然生出纵横天地的心，化茧成蝶。

让"译趣坊系列"也带你飞。

张白桦

2020 年大暑于塞外古城

图书在版编目（CIP）数据

世界有时残酷　但爱从未缺席：英汉对照/（墨西哥）阿普里尔·温特斯等著；张白桦译.—北京：中国国际广播出版社，2021.5
（译趣坊.世界微型小说精选）
ISBN 978-7-5078-4889-2

Ⅰ.①世… Ⅱ.①阿…②张… Ⅲ.①小小说－小说集－墨西哥－现代－汉、英 Ⅳ.①I731.45

中国版本图书馆CIP数据核字（2021）第064477号

世界有时残酷　但爱从未缺席（中英双语）

著　　者	［墨西哥］阿普里尔·温特斯 等
译　　者	张白桦
策　　划	张娟平
责任编辑	笑学婧
校　　对	张　娜
设　　计	国广设计室

出版发行	中国国际广播出版社 ［010-83139469　010-83139489（传真）］
社　　址	北京市西城区天宁寺前街2号北院A座一层
	邮编：100055
印　　刷	环球东方（北京）印务有限公司

开　　本	880×1230　1/32
字　　数	145千字
印　　张	7.75
版　　次	2021年6月　北京第一版
印　　次	2021年6月　第一次印刷
定　　价	35.00元

版权所有　盗版必究